In the development of this novel the author was inspired in part by actual events. Having made this clarification it is important to emphasize the fact that this is a work of fiction and the situations described, as well as the characters and their actions are totally imaginary.

Having reviewed the manuscript, as required by law, the CIA requires the following disclaimer:

The Dead Lawyer

Copyright © 2017 by Michael R. Davidson.

MRD Enterprises, Inc.
PO BOX 1000
Mount Jackson, VA 22844
mrdenter@shentel.net

Library of Congress Control Number: 2017915976
ISBN-13: 978-0692967669
ISBN-10: 0692967664

Contact author at info@michaelrdavidson.com

Cover by Damonza

Printed and bound in the United States of America.

First printing 2017
Second printing 2020

Also by Michael R. Davidson

Harry's Rules

Eye for an Eye

Incubus

The Incubus Vendetta

The Inquisitor and the Maiden

Retribution

Krystal

The Dead Lawyer

Spilled Blood

The Dove

A Peculiar Profession

With Kseniya Kirillova

In the Shadow of Mordor

Successor

A Krystal Murphy Mystery

THE DEAD LAWYER

FOREWORD

Mikhail Illarionovich Kutuzov led the Russian Armies during the Napoleonic invasion of his fatherland. In the late 1950's his nation chose to honor him by giving his name to a major thoroughfare in Moscow. Some old Soviet luminaries used to live in luxury apartments along the way: Brezhnev, Suslov, Andropov.   These were names to make men's knees shake during the dark period of Communist rule.   The eastern end of the avenue is especially affluent, even today, including the Dorogomilovo District.

The broad avenue is heavily traveled, but on a dark, freezing night in January there was not so much traffic.   The Ukraine Hotel with its grandiose Stalinesque tower sits on the north side of the avenue at its far eastern limit, just before one reaches the Novoarbatskiy Bridge leading across the Moskva River into the Arbat District.

On this particular night a darkened car with a single occupant was parked in the hotel's parking lot facing the avenue.   The occupant nervously drummed his fingers on the steering wheel as the seconds ticked by.   At a pre-arranged time, a second car drove past the hotel in the direction of the bridge.   As the second car drove past the driver pressed a button on the small device in the seat beside him.   The device emitted a signal that activated a similar device in the first car, and an electronic "handshake" was initiated.   During the few seconds of that contact a series of compressed digital signals passed between the devices.

A green light on the device indicted that the contact had been made, and the first car slowly exited the parking lot and drove west. The second car continued across the bridge into the Arbat District. Once across the bridge the driver continued a short distance on Konyushkovaya Street before turning into Bol'shoy Devyatinskiy Lane where the American Embassy is located.

CHAPTER 1

The sound was lost in the damp, misted air. It was more like a pop, repeated twice in quick succession, than a bang, and no one heard besides the man who pulled the trigger. He turned calmly and limped away, his face turned downward, and was swallowed by the mist and the darkness.

Detective Lieutenant Krystal Murphy is obstinate, has a thin skin and a hot Irish temper she struggles to control. She is admittedly a difficult person, and she is intelligent enough to recognize it. These traits are known universally within the Arlington County Police Department and despite them or perhaps thanks to them, she had attained the position of head of the Robbery/Homicide Unit. She sometimes wondered if it was stubborn persistence over the years of fighting misogyny and butting heads or the fact that she was really good at her job that got her through it all.

She should have been content with success, and confident in her abilities, such as they are measured in that particular police department. Arlington County, Virginia, which stretches along the Potomac directly opposite Washington, DC, is not exactly a hotbed of crime. She was restless and vaguely dissatisfied, conditions that might be attributed to loneliness. It wasn't that she was bored with her work, but she was beginning to feel that she needed a change.

It was either that or add smoking to an already borderline problem with alcohol. People seemed to enjoy cigarettes, but the habit had earned a grotty reputation, so why pile on another bad habit? Had she been a man, she thought, she would probably take up cigars. Ray Velazquez enjoyed the occasional cheroot and likened knowledge of the tobacco leaf to that of wine connoisseurs.

Ray was her boyfriend. Boyfriend? The word had a juvenile jangle against her inner ear. So, what was he? Lover? Most certainly that. But it was a long-distance relationship, and that made it ... complicated, another source of her discontent.

Ray lived in Miami, and their all too infrequent rendezvous began with fierce passion and ended with unspoken mutual resentment that they must part again. It had become a pattern – joy at the beginning, frustration at the end. She wondered if Ray was being unfaithful to her between visits. With an out of town "girlfriend," he would have plenty of opportunity in swinging Miami.

Ray drove a red Porsche confiscated from a drug dealer, and kept a surprisingly neat apartment in Coconut Grove. He was a cop, too, and she owed him her life – not figuratively but literally. He had nearly died in the process.

With all this roiling in her head she slept only fitfully.

The unwelcome buzz of a cell phone in the hours when people should be sleeping is a disturbance all too familiar to police officers. Accidents and crime do not adhere to a nine-to-five schedule. Krystal Murphy opened her eyes and squinted at her watch which informed her that it was two A.M. She felt like she hadn't slept at all.

She groaned and sat up and rested her feet on the cool floor. It was early spring, and the nights were still chilly. She let the phone ring a few more times while she enjoyed the cool sensation on the soles of her feet and collected her wits. The throbbing in her temples made her wish she had abstained from that second scotch before hitting the sack. When she felt fully awake she snatched the pulsing cell phone from the bedside table. The caller ID. confirmed that it was the Arlington County Police dispatcher.

"What is it?"

"Sorry to wake you, detective, but they found a body out at the Washington Country Club."

The club's name is a hold-over from its founding in the 19th Century when the south bank of the Potomac was still part of the District of Columbia. It is located off Glebe Road near the northern boundary of Arlington County's twenty-six square miles.

She calculated the distance and said, "Tell them I'll be there in about thirty minutes, and make sure no one touches anything. Send a couple of patrol cars out there to tape off the crime scene."

Unlike the District of Columbia there are few homicides in Arlington County, an irony in that Virginia is a strong Second Amendment state while the District prohibits handguns. The more affluent northern sections of the county are statistically the safest, with violent crime near the bottom of the scale.

Housing is varied throughout the county; a lot of it old, but with an average price tag of nearly $700,000 and cost of living 40% above the national average, so the low crime rate is no surprise. It's a bedroom community in the constantly expanding, recession-proof megalopolis around Washington. The counties surrounding the nation's capital are among the richest in the country, and they will stay that way as long as they can suckle at Washington's free-flowing teats. Krystal could barely manage the rent on her small apartment on a cop's wages.

So, a body at the country club was statistically unlikely to be a murder victim. Nevertheless, when an unusual death occurs, Krystal is the one called to the scene.

Most of her time was spent on robberies, but she was not unfamiliar with murder cases, having been at the center of the most spectacular such cases in recent memory. One had ended with a crooked Commonwealth Attorney dead and the Chief of the Criminal Investigations Section wounded at Krystal's hand. The latter was serving a long sentence in a federal penitentiary.

An earlier case that involved international intrigue at the highest level had seen her knocked unconscious and thrown into the trunk of a car by a serial killer.

Given such notoriety it was only natural that Murphy should be viewed with a mixture of awe and fear by the 350 members of the force, especially those above her in the chain of command. Senior officers are uncomfortable with subordinates who have become "untouchable" through remarkable circumstances. It made Murphy uncomfortable, as well, another reason for her discontent.

For both personal and professional reasons Miami beckoned. At another level entirely, the FBI had tried to recruit her, but she didn't feel comfortable with the feebies. She was a street cop at heart.

Compared with her recent experiences, the infrequency of interesting cases grated on her. She had welcomed challenges her entire life, if the truth be known, sought them out. Her brother had never left the family farm back in Indiana, and she sometimes envied his contentment. Life was a series of tests, and Murphy didn't know whether she or her brother had come up with the best answer.

She went to the bathroom, splashed some water on her face and brushed her teeth before donning her standard uniform consisting of a dark blue Arlington County Police polo shirt, jeans and sneakers. In a nod to the coolness of the night she added a light-weight jacket and a baseball cap with a badge embroidered above the bill. She pulled her shoulder length auburn hair into a ponytail. Last, she clipped her Beretta and holster onto her belt, clipped cuffs behind her back, and hung her shield around her neck.

A half-hour later she pulled her unmarked black Dodge Challenger into the parking lot in front of the sprawling whitewashed main building of the country club. A light rain had begun to fall, and the flashing blue and red strobes of the cop cars punched through the accompanying mist and refracted through the drops on the windshield.

Three cop cars were parked in a rough semi-circle so their headlights shone on a late model coupe and reflected off the wet pavement. The mist caught the light and rendered the car into a hazy object of mystery, as though it had just materialized from nothing. The effect was spoiled by the yellow crime scene tape strung all around. A light cloud of exhaust showed that the car's engine was still running, but the lights were off.

She was pleased to see that no one was inside the tape. The uniforms sheltered from the rain in their cars waiting for her. The mobile forensics unit had not yet arrived. When they did they'd set up Klieg lights. But even they knew she would want to examine the scene first. At least, no one would argue with her.

Glad she had worn a cap and jacket, she walked up to one of the black and whites and was pleased to see Sergeant Frank Watson behind the wheel. Watson was a senior uniform and like Krystal and many other members of the force was former military. Both had served in the Military Police in Iraq. He had been her supervisor in Arlington when she was a rookie.

The tall, gangly Georgia native unlimbered from the car and pulled on his visored cap. "Hi, Red. Miserable night to be called out." He looked upward as the rain increased intensity. Frank was the only member of the Arlington County Police who dared call Krystal Red. He was as close to a real friend on the force that she had.

"Aren't they all? What have we got, Frank?"

"Dead guy's in the car over there." He waved laconically toward the late model BMW 3-series dimly illuminated in the parking lot lights. "The night watchman discovered him about an hour ago. It ain't pretty. Looks like he was shot in the head, and more than once. It ain't no suicide for sure."

Watson's grammar was more for effect than indicative of his level of education. Krystal knew how smart he really was, and his easy-going folksiness put people at ease.

"Any other witnesses?"

"Nope. The guard called the club President after he notified us. He's on his way, I think."

"Who's the vic?"

"Don't know yet for sure, but the car's registered to the Dillon Law Offices."

She recognized the name. Dillon was one of the highest-octane law firms in the county. She had the vague recollection that they handled big corporate accounts rather than criminal law.

"Let's go take a look," she said, and crossed under the tape with Watson following.

The BMW's engine was idling, and the driver's side window was open. The dead man slumped in the seat restrained by the seat belt. His head, what was left of it, lolled to one side. The skull literally had been split open by the force of high powered bullets. Krystal showed her flashlight over the car's interior and saw that it was splattered liberally with congealing blood and brain matter. Damage to the head made identification impossible, but the victim had been a young man, well-dressed in a suit and tie. There was probably a wallet with ID. on the body, but its position in the car ruled out a quick search. She would have to wait for forensics to go over the scene and remove the body.

Krystal showed her light on the ground and

R. Davidson**

under the car. "I don't see any shell casings," she said to Watson. "Did one of your guys pick them up?"

"Are you kidding? Nobody's touched anything per your orders." He was slightly put out by the question.

"Sorry," she said, "just making sure."

She scanned the parking lot and the long, white façade of the club's sprawling main building and spotted two closed circuit television cameras that covered the area. She pointed at one of them and said, "Make sure the club president knows we'll need the recordings from those cameras."

"Sho 'nuff," drawled Watson.

She made a circuit of the victim's car. With no eye witnesses to question, there was little more she could do until the CCTV video was available and the victim was identified.

The fact that the victim was still in the driver's seat with his seat belt fastened and engine idling meant that he had either just arrived or was just leaving the parking lot when he had been killed. The driver's side window had been lowered before shots were fired. She'd checked that the glass had not been shattered. This suggested that the victim knew his killer.

"What time did the night guard say he found the body?"

"Around one A.M.," replied Watson.

"I wonder what time the club closes."

"I already checked that," said Watson. "Guard says they close at 10:30 week nights, and the staff is usually all gone within an hour after that."

"What time does the guard go on duty?"

10

"I asked that, too. They don't have an armed guard during the day, and the night guy gets here just before 10:30 on week nights and checks all the doors and windows after closing."

"So, I'm betting he found the body on his first round outside the building?"

"Yup. That's what he said."

"So, the murder must have occurred sometime between 10:30 and 1:00 A.M. when he came upon the scene."

"Seems like."

She looked around again as the rain began to fall harder. "Better get a tarp over the car," she said, "before the rain gets into that open window and washes away evidence."

Watson looked up at the gathering sky. "Pretty soon it'll be raining like a cow pissing on a flat rock."

What the hell could she say to that?

There was no way yet to know whether the victim was a member of the club or even if it would make any difference. It was an unusual place for a murder. What had the victim been doing in the empty parking lot of a country club that had been closed hours before?

She sheltered from the rain in her car while Watson supervised the placement of a tarp over the BMW's open window. The forensics van should arrive at any moment and she wanted to talk to the technician before leaving. A glance at her watch told her it was nearing 3:30 A.M. She decided to return to her apartment after speaking with the tech. It would be some time before the evidence could be processed.

There would be no more sleep, but a hot shower

and a fresh change of clothes would be welcome. She'd grab breakfast at Bob & Edith's Diner, an unpretentious 24-hour place she'd discovered close to her apartment. She'd need sustenance for the day she envisioned.

CHAPTER 2

Krystal arrived at Police Headquarters at 6:30 A.M. She'd lingered over breakfast with a second and then a third cup of black coffee. She'd ordered one of her favorites, sausage gravy on biscuits topped with a pair of over-easy eggs and a side of home fries. Her normal morning fare was a go-cup of Starbucks latte grabbed on the way to work, but given the morning's events she didn't know when she might eat again that day.

Headquarters is in a large, modern concrete and glass building at 1425 North Courthouse Road that houses the county court, as well as the police. Conveniently located next door is the Arlington County Detention Facility.

She was gratified to see that Forensics had been busy. Someone dropped off a packet of crime scene photos that made the body look even worse in the glare of bright lights. The ID had been on the body. The victim's name was Dugan Dillon, age 32, with a residence in McLean, Virginia.

The personal effects were in a separate envelope and included a Van Cleef & Arpel wrist watch, keys, some change, a wallet, and a cell phone. Krystal was especially interested in the latter, but the fact that the valuables had not been taken suggested something altogether more sinister and complicated than a simple robbery gone bad.

The BMW was registered to the Dillon law firm, and it was natural to suspect that the victim was a lawyer. In her experience, any crime involving lawyers spelled trouble with a capital 'T.' The vic's name suggested even more complications of a political nature.

Dugan Dillon was too young to be a principal at the firm, but he was certainly related. The first order of business would be to inform the family, and that unpleasant task fell to Krystal and had to be done as soon as possible. She wanted to check out the cell phone, but notifying next of kin was always at the head of the list.

The address was on Walden Drive, an affluent neighborhood of million dollar plus homes with picture perfect, professionally landscaped lawns in McLean, Virginia. The rain had given way to a bright spring morning as Krystal pulled her car into the driveway. The two-car garage door was open. One bay was empty, presumably where the BMW normally would be, and in the other was a Mercedes SUV. The trip had cost over an hour in Northern Virginia's hectic rush-hour traffic.

She sat in the car for a minute calming herself. Delivering a death notification was never easy, and no matter how many times Krystal had done it, it never got any easier. She had to steel her reaction to the family's sorrow, but stoicism had never been a strong part of her Irish character.

The front door of the house opened as she stepped out of the car, and a woman who looked to be in her mid to late twenties emerged with an anxious look at the unmarked, but unmistakable police car. She wore a terry robe over pajamas, and judging from her appearance, she had had no more sleep than Krystal.

"Mrs. Dillon?" Krystal was wearing her normal work clothes, jeans and an Arlington County Police polo shirt. Her shield and weapon were clearly visible.

The woman's eyes widened in alarm. "Yes."

Krystal identified herself and softening her voice asked, "May we go inside? We need to sit down before we talk."

"Oh, God!" The woman broke into tears and seemed about to collapse as Krystal took both her arms and led her gently inside.

They passed through a marble-floored foyer into the living room where Krystal guided the woman to a sofa. It was a nice living room with a white carpet. Who in their right mind has a white carpet?

Krystal knelt on the floor in front of her. "You are Dugan Dillon's wife?"

"Y-yes. I'm Katherine Dillon."

"Are you alone here?"

"No. Our children are upstairs ... with their nanny."

This was good. She should have thought to bring someone with her. "I'm afraid I have difficult news, Mrs. Dillon. Your husband was found dead in his car early this morning."

Katherine Dillon seemed to stop breathing for a few beats, and her tear reddened eyes fixed on the police detective. She began to shake before burying her face in her hands.

A sturdily built middle-aged woman with dark hair appeared at the door. She looked Latin, and unlike Katherine Dillon, she was fully dressed. Krystal guessed this was the nanny.

"I'm detective Murphy. What's your name?"

Her eyes never leaving her employer, the woman said, "Mercedes, Mercedes Undurraga. What has happened?" Her English was good, but with a strong accent.

"Mr. Dillon is dead." Krystal thought she might have phrased it less abruptly. "Can you please get a glass of water for Mrs. Dillon?"

Mercedes' hand flew to her mouth. "Oh, *Dios mio*," she exclaimed. "Of course, right away." And she scurried out of sight to return a few moments later with the water. She placed the glass on the low table in front of the sofa and stood back nervously. "Is there anything else I can do?"

"Have you been here all night with Mrs. Dillon?" asked Krystal.

"Yes, of course."

She turned to Katherine. "Is there someone I can call to come be with you?"

Katherine was struggling to control her emotions. "Yes. His father needs to know what's happened. P-Paul Dillon."

She recited the number in a mechanical voice, and Krystal wrote it down in her notebook. She wanted to get the answers to a few questions before making the call. She had a feeling that with the senior Dillon present, answers might not be forthcoming.

"Mrs. Dillon, can you tell me about the last time you saw your husband?"

Katherine stared at her uncomprehendingly, and Krystal repeated the question.

With a nervous glance at the nanny, she said, "It was last night. He received a call very late. We'd already gone to bed."

"Can you recall the hour?"

"It must have been around 10:30 or 11."

"Who was it who called?"

"I-I don't know. Dugan said he had to go somewhere and got dressed right away."

"Do you think it was someone he knew?"

"He didn't say. I asked what was going on, but he wouldn't say. Just that it was important."

"Did he have any enemies?"

The nanny stepped behind the sofa and placed her hands on her employer's shoulders.

Katherine looked confused. "Everybody loved Dugan."

It was a standard initial next-of-kin interview. For the time being the wife could be eliminated as a suspect, but that could change. If the nanny were to be believed, the wife could not have pulled the trigger, but there were other ways she could be involved.

She asked Mercedes Undurraga to step into the kitchen so they could speak separately. As someone who lived in the house, she would likely know about any family problems or disagreements. But the woman could offer no more than already had been said.

Katherine Dillon was either unable or unwilling to say if anything had been bothering her husband. "Dugan didn't bring things like that home from the office," she'd said. He'd canceled their weekly dinner at his father's home last week was all she had to say, and she didn't know why.

She would have to have the Dillons' phone records checked to see who had made the call that led Dugan to leave the house at so late an hour. The man's cell phone was waiting on Krystal's desk, too, and it might well provide a solid lead.

CHAPTER 3

It was after 10:00 A.M. and the traffic heading toward D.C. along the parkway reminded her of a closely packed shoal of fish. She decided to try Military Road instead, but it was glutted, as well, and for a fleeting moment she missed the open roads of sparsely populated southern Indiana where she'd grown up.

A call diverted her at the last minute to the Chief's office. Everett Fogerty, she knew, was on his way out as Chief of Police. He planned to retire within a few months, and his replacement already had been named. She had an uneasy relationship with Fogerty whose attitude toward her was ruled alternately by admiration and resentment of her high public profile.

He looked like a man ready for retirement. This morning there were dark circles under his eyes and a concerned expression on his soft, round face.

"Where have you been, Murphy? I called your office hours ago."

"I just got the message, Chief. I was out in McLean on an interview. We had a murder last night."

Fogerty blinked at her before speaking. "The Dillon murder. You were interviewing the family?"

The Chief knew the drill as well as she, but he was nervous about something.

"Yes, sir. I had to notify the wife and ask a few questions."

"You spoke with the victim's wife?"

Hadn't she just said this? She nodded.

"Was Paul Dillon there?"

"No. But he's been notified and is probably with his daughter-in-law by now."

Fogerty's nervous level dropped a few degrees, and Krystal began to get the picture. Paul Dillon was a bigshot in the county, a powerful man with powerful friends and political connections. She was going to get the "tread lightly" speech.

"Do you know who Paul Dillon is?"

"Vaguely. He heads a big law firm."

"He heads the biggest and most important law practice in the county and he'll be dogging our every action concerning his son's murder. He has a lot of friends in high places in Richmond and Washington. I think he's a personal friend of the Governor."

"Of course." She didn't succeed in keeping the sarcasm out of her voice.

Fogerty gave her a sharp look. "He wants to see me this afternoon, and I want you to go with me. He'll want to know everything we've found out so far."

"We don't know very much, Chief. I haven't even had time to check all the evidence."

"Well, you'd better have something to tell him. He won't expect us to be handling this as a run of the mill case."

The remark pricked Krystal's thin, Irish skin. "You know that's not so, Chief. What material evidence there is landed on my desk just before I had to go make the death notification to Dugan Dillon's wife. There are several things I have to look at before I can even start to draw conclusions. Don't you think it would be better to postpone meeting the father, at least for a day?"

"You don't refuse a request from Paul Dillon.

We'll meet him this afternoon at one o'clock. You need to have your ducks in a row by then. Meet me in front of the Navy League Building on Clarendon Boulevard at 12:45."

Krystal looked at her watch, and the look on her face made it clear she was unhappy. It was already after eleven.

As she turned to leave Fogerty said, "And be sure to wear something more appropriate."

She bit her tongue and stalked out of the office without a word. She'd have to go to her apartment to change which meant there would literally be no time to thoroughly check the victim's cell phone and follow up on whatever she would find. At least she could order a check on Dugan Dillon's home phone. She wanted to know who had made that call to him last night. It had very likely been his murderer.

The Dillon Law Offices were located in a multi-story concrete building on Arlington's main drag, Clarendon Boulevard along with a lot of other businesses. The county is a rough rectangle with straight line boundaries on two sides recalling the time it was part of the District of Columbia, and bounded on the long side by the Potomac River and ending in an irregular bulge to encompass Reagan National Airport. Route 1, leading to the airport is densely developed and lined with hotels. It has a heavy Federal Government presence in the Pentagon, Arlington National Cemetery, and the small group of glass towers in Rosslyn's Crystal City where Key Bridge crosses the river to Georgetown.

Krystal found Chief Fogerty pacing back and forth in front of the doors. He wore a freshly pressed uniform. She'd changed into a demure, dark blue pant suit, white silk blouse, and low heels. The suit did not lend itself to carrying her Beretta, so she'd tucked her .380 Smith & Wesson into her waistband under her jacket.

Fogerty looked her up and down and nodded approval before leading her into the building to the elevators.

The law office spaces left no doubt that the firm was prosperous. There was a lot of rich wood panelling, and tasteful oil paintings festooned the walls. On the wall behind the receptionist were framed photos of the principles. Larger than the rest was a picture of a middle-aged man with well-coifed silver hair who must be the head of the firm.

Fogerty announced them, and the receptionist made a quick call on the intercom and led them through a series of hallways to a heavy wooden door. She knocked lightly and opened the door into a magnificent office with a lot of polished wood and brass dominated by a huge desk. The silver-haired man who rose from behind the desk wore a bespoke suit. Unlike his photo, Paul Dillon wore black horn-rimmed glasses which he removed and placed in his breast pocket as he rose and strode forward to meet them.

"Chief Fogerty, thank you so much for coming. I'm Paul Dillon," he said as he stretched his hand to the Chief. His voice was low and soft. He looked inquiringly at Krystal.

"Mr. Dillon, this is Detective Lieutenant Krystal

Murphy. She's heading our investigation. We're very sorry for your loss."

Dillon eyed her with interest and extended his hand. His grasp was firm and dry. "Detective," he said, "thank you for coming."

There were a pair of leather covered high-backed chairs and a sofa placed around a low table at one end of his office in front of a wall of law books. One of the walls on the side was festooned with photos of Dillon with well-known people, many of whom Krystal recognized as politicians. Such displays are known as vanity walls, and in Washington you are nobody if you don't have one like a Sioux brave with no scalps. Paul Dillon invited them to take seats. She and Fogerty settled onto the sofa, and Dillon took one of the chairs.

"May I offer you some coffee or tea? Mineral water?" he asked.

Fogerty coughed nervously. "No, thank you, sir. As I said, we are deeply sorry for your loss, and I want to assure you personally that we will bend every effort to identifying the, er, perpetrator."

"Thank you, Chief Fogerty." Dillon looked back and forth between them, letting his gaze rest finally on Krystal. "I believe I've read something about you, Detective. You were involved in that unfortunate business concerning the State's Attorney, correct? What a shame. I knew Sara Hampton well."

"Yes, sir," nodded Krystal. "It was very unfortunate." She wanted to start asking questions herself and was surprised that Dillon would indulge in small talk.

"What can you tell me about what happened?"

asked Dillon, addressing Krystal rather than the Chief.

"I've not had time yet to look at all the physical evidence." She shot a weighted glance at Fogerty. "As you know, I visited your daughter-in-law this morning."

She related the details of the crime as circumspectly as possible. "There is no doubt we're dealing with a cold-blooded murder, sir, and anything you might know or even suspect that may have a bearing would be very useful to our investigation."

"This matter is the Department's number one priority, I assure you," interjected Fogerty.

Dillon ignored him, keeping his attention on Krystal. "Anything I can do to help," he said. "What do you want to know?"

"As yet we have no motive and no identified suspects," said Krystal. She took out her notebook and pen and gave Dillon an expectant look. "It's possible that a case your son was working on is the reason. Has there been a problem in that regard, a resentful client, for example?"

"Not that I'm aware."

Krystal thought he had answered a little too quickly. Dillon must have thought through such possibilities beforehand.

"He had no personal enemies you know about?" she persisted.

"Dugan was well-liked by everyone. He was a nice guy." Dillan's voice caught in his throat when he said this, the first sign of emotion since they'd met him.

"Would it be possible to look over his recent cases? There might be something in the files."

Dillon's face registered slight alarm. "Dugan's cases were the firm's cases, Detective, and are subject to attorney-client privilege. I'm not sure I could permit free rein to comb through them. Even under these circumstances we must protect the interests of our clients."

Krystal was reminded of why she disliked lawyers.

She frowned. "Mr. Dillon, at this point in the investigation any hint, the smallest bit of information that may show us a path to the guilty party will help. What case was Dugan working on most recently?"

"Um, he handled several corporate clients. These aren't cases that involve any particular individual."

Corporations, Krystal knew, were made up of individuals with very particular interests.

"Well," she said, "I hope you will reconsider. We need all the help we can get right now."

"I'll think about it," said Dillon.

He stood to indicate the meeting was over. "Thank you, Chief Fogerty, and you, too, Detective Murphy, for this kindness. I hope you'll be able to keep me informed of any progress."

Fogerty was quick to answer. "Of course, Mr. Dillon." He leapt to his feet anxious to leave before Krystal could say anything else. "Detective Murphy will keep you fully informed."

Krystal put away her notebook. She'd not filled even one page.

They shook hands again, but as they were about to leave Dillon said, "Chief, would you mind a few words in private?"

Krystal was left in the hallway to find her way back to the reception area to wait. What could Dillon want to say to Fogerty that he couldn't say in front of the officer in charge of the investigation of his son's murder? She took several deep breaths to tamp down her ire.

Ten minutes later Fogerty reappeared, and they rode the elevator down in silence. The Chief was lost in thought and refused to look at her.

Back on the street she said, "Well, that was a total waste of time. That guy was less than forthcoming. What did he say after he kicked me out?"

Fogerty turned on her. "Murphy, the man did not 'kick you out.' He's just lost his son. This was a courtesy call on a grieving family member and he wanted the reassurance of the Chief of Police that we were on the case. Make sure you keep me in the loop on everything you find." And he stomped away to his waiting car and driver.

Krystal was dumbfounded. Cooperation was in scarce supply today. The two people who should most want to help her were treating her like a redheaded stepchild. She wondered if Paul Dillon might be dissatisfied that a woman was in charge of the investigation. She'd run into that prejudice more than once.

Back at her desk she confirmed that the records from Dugan Dillon's home phone had been requested. It would be at least a day before they would be available. In the meantime, she picked up Dugan's cell phone and began poking the keys. The call logs were empty. Dugan had evidently cleared the memory recently. Why would he have done that? There were about three hundred photos, all of them of family at home or on vacation. The contacts list was long but offered no immediate clues. Maybe later when other evidence turned up, one of the contacts would prove important. For now, all she could do was put in another request that the cell phone provider hand over the call logs. That left her with no trail to follow and no information beyond what she already knew: somebody had murdered Dugan Dillan with two bullets to the brain on a wet night in an empty parking lot.

She remembered the video recordings from the country club.

She called Frank Watson. She hated to bother him because he had been on duty all night and was probably still asleep, but his wife said he was up and put him on the line immediately.

"Frank, sorry to bother you, but did you get the CCTV video from the club last night?"

"The recorder was locked up tight, and the club president said he didn't have the key. He promised to get them this morning. Ain't anyone got them to you yet?"

"No. I haven't seen them."

"Damn. They must still be at the club then. I'll git out there right now."

"I can send someone else, Frank. You need to rest."

"Hell," he said, "I'm off rotation for a couple days. Ain't got nuthin better to do."

This gave her an idea. The other detectives in the unit were all busy with robberies and muggings, and she needed someone to do some footwork and bounce ideas off. She had a lot of confidence in the Georgian, and they got along well. If this was the "number one case" for the Department, Fogerty could not refuse her request for some help.

"Okay, Frank. Go on out there and get the recordings. Then bring them to my office."

"Sho 'nuff, Detective."

She called Fogerty and secured his permission to detach Watson to her for the duration of the case. "Just get it solved quickly," was the Chief's only comment.

Thanks, Chief, she said to herself, *I'd been thinking of taking a few days off.*

Two hours passed before Watson sauntered into her office and handed her an envelope containing two CD-ROM discs. She'd been growing impatient before she remembered that Watson lived far out near the border with West Virginia.

Watson was dressed in jeans, boots, a t-shirt, and carried a helmet under one arm. He also had a red bandanna wrapped around his head. He must have ridden his motorcycle. He possessed an old Harley of which he was quite proud. He whistled softly. "Hey, Red," he said, "you clean up real good."

She'd not bothered to change back into her normal "uniform."

"You look good, too, for a cracker," she replied. "Hey, how would you like to be a detective for a while? I just got Fogerty to assign you to me for the duration of this case."

Watson grinned broadly. "I always wanted to be a detective. When do we start?"

"Right now. Let's take a look at this video."

She slipped the first disc into her computer, and the screen came to life. "Let's start at 10:30 PM."

The disc whirred in the drive and fast forwarded to the desired time. The parking lot was lighted, and the cars of late diners were leaving. One car arrived which must have been the night guard, and only it and the cleaning crew's panel truck remained. The five members of the crew left the building at 11:30 and drove away. Shortly thereafter, the lights illuminating the lot went out. A few exterior lights on the building itself remained on.

"Shit," said Krystal. "They turn the lights out at night?" Then she recalled arriving at the lot and the cop cars' lights shining on the BMW.

"It was like that when we arrived," said Watson.

"Well, let's keep watching. We might get lucky."

"Even a one-eyed hog sometimes finds an acorn," Watson applied one of his well-worn aphorisms. "But not always," he added.

The time track on the recording showed 11:20 when Dugan Dillon's BMW rolled into the lot. He pulled into the space where the car had been found but didn't get out. He was waiting for someone.

After five minutes a lone figure could be seen walking into the lot. It had not yet begun to rain heavily, and his outline was clear. It was a man wearing a short coat and brimmed hat. He walked up to Dugan's car and rapped on the side window. As soon as the window wound down there were two flashes as the weapon discharged. The man stood beside the car for a moment and then turned and hurried out of the lot. Krystal noticed that as the man picked up his pace he limped noticeably on his left leg.

She switched off the computer and swung her chair around to face Watson who had been watching over her shoulder. "Well, detective," she said, "here's what we know: it was murder for sure, and a pre-calculated one – there was no hesitation before the shots, and he probably had the gun already in his hand when he got to the car, the killer was a male with a limp, and Dugan Dillan probably knew him. At least he rolled the window down without hesitation. He wasn't expecting the gun."

"The shooter didn't pick up any brass," said Watson. "So, he used a revolver, a big one judging from the damage it did, probably a .357 or something heavier."

"They should have performed the autopsy by the end of the day out at Manassas," said Krystal. "At least we'll have the type of weapon nailed down. I don't think it'll give us much else."

Manassas, some thirty miles southwest of Arlington, is the location of the Northern Virginia office of the Virginia medical examiner system, charged with investigating all violent deaths in the Commonwealth.

Watson sat in the chair in front of her desk and stretched out his long legs. "Well, as things stand now that'll be about as handy as a pocket on the back of a shirt," he said, "So what do we do next, boss?"

"We get down on our hands and knees and sniff around."

"A hound dog needs a scent to follow. I don't smell nuthin yet." Krystal rolled her eyes. Sometimes Watson overdid it with the good old boy stuff.

"I think we need to talk to the wife again. Maybe we'll pick up a 'scent' there. Do you have any civilian clothes that don't make you look like someone in a biker gang?"

He pretended to be insulted. "Hey, boss, this is me. You think I should change my style?"

"Go home and go through your closet to see if you have anything in there besides uniforms and biker leathers. Meet me here first thing in the morning."

CHAPTER 4

The Mercedes SUV was still in the garage, but another car, a heavy Lexus sedan was in the driveway. The Lexus looked like a lawyer's car, and Krystal wondered if Paul Dillon was inside with his daughter-in-law.

"Damn. I was hoping to catch her alone."

Watson was in the passenger seat next to her looking simultaneously out of place and strangely spruce in a dark brown suit and tie. By contrast, Krystal was back in her habitual jeans and polo shirt.

They rang the bell and were greeted by the nanny, Mercedes, who rolled her eyes like a frightened calf when she saw who it was.

Katherine Dillon appeared from somewhere at the back of the house. She nervously waved them into the living room where an older woman sat reading a newspaper.

Katherine did not invite them to sit.

"This is my mother-in-law, Nancy Dillon," said Katherine, and she introduced the two cops. Nancy rose to her feet and eyed them suspiciously.

"I don't know what more I can tell you." Katherine was nervous. "Do you have some new information?"

"I'm afraid not," replied Krystal.

The older woman spoke. "Then why are you here?"

The nanny, Mercedes Undurraga, appeared at the door and stood silently as she exchanged a glance with Katherine.

Krystal kept her attention on Katherine. "Mrs. Dillon, you've had some time now to reflect on what happened. Maybe something has occurred to you since we spoke last."

Katherine looked blank for a moment. "I can't think of anything that would help," she said. "I think I've told you everything."

Krystal persisted, "Is it possible that Dugan was ... attacked ... because of something he was working on at the law firm?"

Nancy Dillon put an arm around Katherine's shoulder and said, "If you believe it was because of something he was working on you should ask his father. Katherine would know nothing about that."

Krystal's frustration was mounting. No one directly involved seemed willing or able to provide even the most obscure information that might bear on a motive for Dugan Dillon's murder, even those who should have the strongest reasons to help.

Ignoring Nancy, she said, "Are you sure you've scoured your memory for everything. Dugan might have mentioned something in passing, in a casual conversation, that something was bothering him."

Again, a blank stare from Katherine and a hostile one from her mother-in-law.

"Someone called him late at night, after you'd gone to bed. He didn't say anything, at all, before he left? He offered no explanation?"

"He just got dressed and left."

"Did he say where he was going?"

"No."

"Did he seem particularly worried when he left?"

"No."

"He said nothing at all, just got up, dressed, and left?"

Katherine Dillon nodded mutely. Was there an undertone of obstinacy in her nearly monosyllabic responses? Like a well-rehearsed witness in court she volunteered nothing. And the mother-in-law acted like a guard dog.

Twenty short minutes after they arrived, Krystal and Watson were back in the car.

"That was fast," said Watson. "Do you detectives always run into roadblocks like that?"

Nancy Dillon had accompanied them, actually herded them, to the door underscoring the fact that the meeting was over. She repeated that questions about the family and Dugan's business matters should be directed to Paul Dillon at his office.

Krystal chewed her lip for a beat before answering Watson. "Most victims' families cooperate with the police unless they're guilty themselves. We know that Katherine Dillon didn't shoot her husband, but she has to know more than she's willing to say."

CHAPTER 5

"Just get over it. We all have unsolved cases in the files." Ray Velazquez lifted a thimble-sized cup of sweet Cuban coffee to his lips and drained it.

Nearly two months had elapsed since the Dillon murder, and Krystal had taken advantage of the long Fourth of July weekend to visit Ray in Miami. He had treated her to a seafood lunch at one of his favorite restaurants and then driven them to Little Havana, where they now sat at a small café table on the sidewalk. He replaced the cup on the table and took a drag from a Miami-rolled cigar.

A breeze that slightly mitigated the heat of the Miami sun carried the smoke across the table and Krystal inhaled its sweet fragrance.

She couldn't get the Dillon case out of her mind. She and Watson had run into one dead-end after another, and in a few weeks, it would be officially designated as a cold case. It did not sit well with her.

"Well, I've not had a case go cold yet," she said. "I know we don't have nearly the number of murders you have down here with all you hot-blooded Latinos, but this sticks in my craw."

"That's natural," he said, "but look around." He languidly waved his cigar at peaceful Little Havana, leaving a thin ribbon of smoke as his hand moved through the air. Old guys were playing dominoes, slapping the tiles down hard on card tables set up on the sidewalk, people were walking around, rapid, Cuban-inflected Spanish was in the air. "Relax. You're on holiday; we're together, so let's enjoy it and avoid shop talk."

"I don't want to," she said. "I want your advice. Am I missing something I could do?"

He sighed, "*Dios mío*, you're like a dog that's gnawed all the meat off a bone and keeps looking for more. Sometimes people don't talk. Sometimes they really know something, and sometimes they don't. If you don't get some kind of lucky break, something out of the blue, it's just hard to make any progress. Sometimes it's better to be lucky than good."

"Well, I've not had a shitload of luck in a while."

He feigned hurt. "But, Krystal, you're here. You're with me. What more could a girl want?"

She had to smile. "Yeah, guess I'm a lucky gal, after all."

"*Por cierto*," he smiled back, his teeth brilliant against his tanned skin. Krystal's first impression of him when they'd met two years earlier had been that he looked like something out of the old Miami Vice TV show, an image that was reinforced by his blond, surfer hair and the bright red Porsche 911 cabriolet he drove way too fast through Miami. Today he wore a crisp, white *guayabera* over black jeans and a pair of vintage French *Nautilux* sunglasses. He looked like a damned movie star.

She'd warmed to him quickly and at first brushed off his none too subtle but good-natured attempts to get her into bed. Her resistance to his charms had not lasted awfully long, she reflected, not very long, at all, and this was unusual for her. But they were more than lovers; there was a real friendship there, too. One of Ray's best characteristics, in Krystal's opinion, was that he respected her as a professional. They had bonded in the course of following a trail of tragic murders, and in the end, he had nearly died of a nasty gunshot wound. She nursed him back to health, and a real bond developed. He filled a void in her life she had barely noticed before.

But the distance between Virginia and Florida was slowly pulling them apart. She thought she detected restlessness in Ray, but maybe it was really her own. It was only natural that he should want more than a few scattered moments of her company. It wasn't fair to either of them. Real relationships were permanent, not part-time. They were veering into friends with benefits territory, and she wouldn't blame him if he started looking elsewhere. For all she knew, he already was, though he treated her no differently. She would have to decide soon.

"I feel like a *siesta*," she said.

"Great idea," he grinned, and he wasn't thinking of sleep.

CHAPTER 6

The moment she deplaned in Washington, the cloud of gloom she'd gone to Miami to escape settled over her again. It was as if she suffered from multiple personality disorder. Miami Krystal could relax, enjoy good food, and even laugh with very little prodding from Ray Velazquez. She'd never seen him downcast, and he had a way of lifting her, if only temporarily, to his level of *joie de vivre*. She decided it had a lot to do with his Latin temperament and how carefree things seemed in Miami. Washington and its satellite counties were both sustained and burdened by the weight of the government.

That is not to say there were no happy people there. The megalopolis enjoyed the benefits of wealth and stability, good schools and numerous cultural attractions. But although Washington was supposed to represent the nation, it was a bubble with little in common with the rest of the country, least of all the heartland where Krystal had been raised. Maybe that was it. Maybe that was why she so frequently felt like a fish out of water. Then again, maybe it was just her nature.

"Hey, Red, got a minute?" Frank Watson poked his head through the door. He had returned to uniformed duty weeks before.

Krystal looked up from the scattered crime reports that covered her desk. Any relief from the routine was welcome. "Sure. What's up?"

Frank sank into a chair in front of her desk with that lazy grin of his. The guy could look relaxed in any situation, she thought. But there was something on his mind.

"Ever heard of a website called 'All the Truth'?" he asked.

"It's a muckraking outfit, isn't it? Lots of fake news?"

"Well," he drawled, "maybe sometimes, but it's kinda fun to follow, and it has a large following on the web. Why don't you bring it up on your computer?"

"OK," puzzled, she tapped her keyboard, and garish yellow and green banner appeared at the top of her screen. She looked up. "Now what?"

"Scroll down until you see a familiar name."

She ran the cursor down the screen until she found the headline he meant. It was unmistakable: *"Dillon Murder Tied to Oppo Research Group."*

A frisson passed down her spine. "What the hell?"

"May be the first break in the Dillon case. Read it."

According to the website, Dugan Dillon had been handling legal matters for the Wakefield Group, an investigative service used by political parties to dig up dirt on opponents, commonly known as "opposition research." The group's name had cropped up in several news accounts of dirty tricks during the current Presidential campaign, including alleged contacts with Russian Intelligence. The website claimed that Dugan Dillon had become suspicious of certain of his client's activities shortly before he was murdered. The Dillon family were heavy political contributors, and the article hinted darkly at back room political mischief.

Ray Velazquez's comment that sometimes it was better to be lucky than good flashed through her mind. "Jeez, the Russians? Sounds crazy"

"Not if you follow the news these days," said Watson.

Politics. Everything in and around Washington revolved around politics. It always muddied the waters, created enemies and allies of convenience, and led to lies, cover-ups, and self-righteous denials.

She checked the list of clients Dugan Dillon had handled for his father's law firm, but the Wakefield Group wasn't on it. Paul Dillon had reluctantly provided the client list, but steadfastly refused to provide any details.

"What do you think?" she asked.

"I suppose Paul Dillon could have made a mistake. On the other hand, he could have left Wakefield off on purpose. He doesn't come off as the kind of guy who'd make mistakes."

"Something like this is more likely to make our job harder than easier," she said.

"Yup, but it's a lead."

"Would you like to play detective again?"

"I'd miss my uniform."

"You clean up good," she mimicked his accent.

Watson laughed and shook his head. "You'd better clear it with the Chief."

Everett Fogerty had retired the month before, and it was the happiest Krystal had ever seen the man. Presumably he was somewhere fishing in the Outer Banks now. His replacement was Daniel Heck. The new Chief was a former officer in the Naval Criminal Investigations Service, and it was possible to admire the man. He was a no-nonsense kind of person and had not yet fallen victim to the politics that swirled around his job. Krystal wondered how long he would last.

Heck read the website report and agreed to attach Watson temporarily to the investigation. "First thing is to find out who wrote this and see what kind of sources he used," said the Chief. "I don't like unsolved cases, Murphy. See if you can breathe some life into it."

"It'll be tricky," she said, "He'll probably invoke some journalistic confidentiality crap."

"Then lean on him. Just don't break any bones."

Krystal liked the Chief even more.

All The Truth's address was a long, single story red brick building that rented offices to a variety of businesses on Union Street overlooking the Potomac in Alexandria. It was fronted by a shiny lobby with two receptionists who directed them to a small suite of offices in the rear of the building.

They knocked on the door and entered without waiting for an invitation. The outer office contained a disorderly mess of cardboard boxes filled with computer parts and old keyboards, newspapers, and other assorted junk. In the midst of the chaos was a skinny, bearded young man in jeans and a Che Guevara T-shirt seated at a metal table with a keyboard and three computer monitors. He was staring with concentration at one of the screens. His name was Leon Trotsky Ames, as they were to learn.

Michael R. Davidson

Ames looked up in surprise at the intrusion, and the surprise turned to slight alarm when Watson, looking dapper again in a light gray suit, flashed his badge.

"It was an accident, I swear," he blurted. "I'll never go to that bar again."

It was an interesting greeting, but not one to which either cop was unaccustomed. A guilty conscience suggested a cooperative interview.

Krystal took the lead. "We'd like to talk to you about something more important than your 'accident.' We're investigating a murder."

Ames gaped at them. His eyes rolled upward as if he were trying to remember whether he'd killed anyone lately.

"Specifically," continued Krystal, "we want to talk to you about the Dugan Dillon murder. Your website carried an article this morning making some pretty specific allegations. Did you write it?"

Now Ames became guarded. He didn't like talking to police, and it showed. "No. I didn't write it."

By this time the conversation had drawn another young man to the door to the connecting office. Like his co-worker, he wore jeans and a T-shirt with a picture of a large bone accompanied by the words "I find this humerus."

He said, "I wrote it."

"And who are you?" asked Watson.

"Alex Apelbaum. I'm the editor."

"Well, Alex Apelbaum," said Krystal, "we need to have a talk with you."

"Come into my office." He waved them through the door into another space quite similar in décor to the first. There was a ratty couch against one wall, and he waved them toward it. "Have a seat." He sat behind his desk.

Apelbaum was clean-shaven and would have been good looking had he not shaved the sides of his head leaving a line of curly hair on top from front to back. He wore an earring in one ear. Krystal wondered why today's youth were so intent on acting like every day was Halloween.

Apelbaum gave them a sly look and asked, "So, what can I do for you?"

"We'd like to talk about the article about Dugan Dillon. You make some serious allegations. We want to know where you got the information."

"I thought so," he said, the sly smirk still on his face. Unlike his colleague, he was enjoying himself.

The walls were plastered with posters extolling the Black Lives Matter movement, Occupy Wall Street, and other exhortations to protest whatever it was popular to be against, which seemed to be just about everything. Apelbaum's anti-establishment political and not particularly law-abiding leanings were evident.

"So," she said, "where did you come up with the material for your story?"

"I'm not sure I can tell you," he said, leaning back in his chair. "Journalistic ethics, you know."

"This is a murder investigation," she persisted, "A helpless man was shot and killed, and he left a wife and two kids. Now we're asking for your help to find his murderer."

"That's all well and good," said Apelbaum, still smiling. "But I have rights, and I don't have to tell you jack shit."

Watson rose from the couch and took two steps to the desk, leaned over into Apelbaum's face, and said, "Son, you look as happy as a dead pig in sunshine, but we have a real problem here. You see, we really care about a widow with two kids and a guy who got his brains spread all over the inside of his car. As far as I'm concerned, if you know somethin' that can help us bring a cold-blooded killer to justice but won't tell us, why you're as guilty as him. I'm sure you'd really like to help, so why don't you just wipe that stupid grin off your face and start talkin'?"

Watson's voice was low and pregnant with menace, and Apelbaum's smile disappeared.

"What are you going to do, beat it out of me?" he said. "Police brutality."

"Son, you ain't seen police brutality. Not yet." Watson reached across the desk and grabbed Apelbaum's shirt, yanking him hard. "Now, Detective Murphy asked you a question. She asked real nice. Maybe she should leave the room for a couple of minutes so I can explain it to you."

Apelbaum turned to Krystal as best he could in Watson's grasp. "OK, OK, I get it. What do you want?"

Watson relaxed his grip but remained leaning over the desk. "Now, boy, you just better remember that the sun don't shine on the same dog's tail all the time, and tell the lady what you know."

Krystal was not certain exactly what Watson's latest utterance meant, but it had an effect. Apelbaum's arrogance disappeared.

"It was a woman," he said. "She called me."

"What's her name," asked Krystal.

"I don't know. She wouldn't tell me. But she

sounded scared, and she seemed to know what she was talking about."

"Don't tell us you went with a story based on information from someone you don't even know." Krystal was incredulous.

Apelbaum recovered some of his confidence. "It was an anonymous source, just like the article said."

Watson shook his head. "So that's what an anonymous source is? Just anyone who calls with any information but won't give a name?"

Apelbaum was defensive. "Well, that's what anonymous means, isn't it?"

"I don't believe you," said Krystal.

Watson glared at Apelbaum who leaned back in his chair as far away from Watson as he could get.

"It's true," said Apelbaum. "I don't know who she is."

"Was it a young voice or an old one?" asked Krystal.

"She sounded young, and she talked real fast."

"Did you record the call?"

"Uh, no."

"If I find out you're lying, we'll be back," she said. "And I'll wait outside while Detective Watson here questions you again."

"I swear it's the truth."

"That outfit makes yellow journalism look like Pulitzer material." Watson lazed in his habitual seat in front of Krystal's desk, legs stretched and ankles crossed.

"Yep. We need to run a background check on

our Mohawked friend. I'll ask for a warrant to check his phone records, but I doubt I'll get one. I think a trip across the river tomorrow morning should be next."

"You want to check out Wakefield?"

"They've probably seen the article, too, so they'll be prepared. But we might find out something."

"How about talking to Paul Dillon again?"

"We'll do that, too."

"Got any ideas about the identity of the anonymous caller?"

"The only young woman we know connected to the case is the widow, Katherine Dillon."

"If it's her, why didn't she tell us the same thing?"

"That's something we need to find out."

CHAPTER 7

Alex Apelbaum and Leon Trotsky Ames had spent the evening in a bar thinking of ways to get even with the bitch cop and her bulldog. Apelbaum was angry, had had too much to drink, but managed to get them home without incident.

He was concentrating on fitting the key to lock the car and not having much luck. Ames, equally drunk and swaying on his feet, was laughing at his failure. Neither of them noticed the car stopping behind them and the door opening. In fact, the car's driver had been following them since they left the offices on Union Street hours earlier.

As Apelbaum fumbled with the key there was a footstep behind them, and he knew nothing else because he was dead already. Ames half turned to see a tall, dark figure with a white face creased by a death's head grin. He staggered back against the car before his face was blown away.

"You see the news this morning?"

Frank Watson's call was early, before Krystal left for the office.

"Yeah, I caught it on the local channel just now."

"Someone's let the fox in the henhouse." Watson just couldn't help himself.

"Yeah, right. We need to reach out to the Alexandria Police." Arlington County's finest have longstanding cooperative relationships with neighboring police throughout the sprawl of Northern Virginia.

According to the news report, Alex Apelbaum and Leon Trotsky Ames had been shot dead at an apartment complex out on Eisenhower Avenue where they shared rooms the night before.

"I don't get it," said Krystal, "Killing Apelbaum is sure to call more attention to the story he wrote."

"Assuming it was connected to the story. Could be something else. He wasn't a very likeable person."

"And he probably pissed off a lot of people with his writing. He didn't have a truckload of ethics."

Krystal pulled the Challenger into a space in front of the modern glass and concrete building that houses the Alexandria Police Department. They had an appointment to see one of the lieutenants in charge of the Criminal Investigation Section who turned out to be a pleasant 40-year-old named Kellog.

The Alexandria cop knew who Krystal was and gave them a warm welcome.

"What can you tell us about the shooting," asked Krystal.

"Not much," said Kellog. "It happened a little after midnight in the parking lot of their apartment building. We haven't found a witness, although some of the residents say they heard what might have been shots."

"Let me guess," said Watson, "Double taps to the head, large calibre?"

Kellog gave them a long look. "That's right.

Large calibre rounds. They made quite a mess."
Kellog shook his head in disgust.

"We can't be sure, but there could be a
connection between this and something we've been
working on for months – the Dillon killing in Arlington.
Same M.O., same kind of weapon."

Kellog raised his eyebrows.

"And," continued Krystal, "we questioned both
of your victims yesterday about the Dillon murder."

This was news to Kellog. They told him about
the article and the interview.

"I agree," said Kellog, "it looks suspicious, and
you're right – there could be no connection between
the article and the killing, but it's something to look
into."

"Do you mind if we take the lead?" asked
Krystal. "We've been working on this for a long time,
and we planned to talk to the people at Wakefield this
morning."

"You'll keep me informed of what you find?
We'll continue the investigation here, of course." said
Kellog, "but so far we have absolutely nothing to go
on."

"Welcome to the club." She didn't mention that
she'd already applied for a warrant to see Apelbaum's
phone records. Kellog would probably do the same,
but this was her case, and she didn't plan to let it go.
Either Apelbaum had known more than he said, or he
hadn't, but whoever killed him thought he did – if the
double murder was connected to the article.

CHAPTER 8

The Wakefield Group's offices were in the District on a high floor in a 'K' Street Northwest highrise just south of the intersection with 17th Street. After nearly an hour fighting traffic begween Alexandria and the District they walked unannounced into the chrome, glass, and marble expanse of the reception area. CCTV cameras sprouted from the walls.

The perky blonde at the counter didn't hide her disapproval of Krystal's jeans and polo shirt, but Krystal didn't care. Of more concern was the huge black man with a shiny shaved head who had risen from a chair near the door when they entered and who took up a position a few paces behind them. Krystal wondered where a man that big found suits to fit.

She pointed to the badge on her belt while Watson flashed his. "We want to speak with George Wakefield," she said.

According to information available on the Internet, George Wakefield spent over thirty years in the CIA before founding his successful consulting firm. There are a lot of people like him scattered in and around Washington, but unlike Wakefield, most are minor players exploiting the remnants of a more rewarding past.

"Mr. Wakefield is very busy," said the receptionist. "Perhaps you would like to make an appointment?"

"We're very busy too," said Krystal, "and we don't have time to make an appointment. We're here on police business, and I suggest you tell him - now."

The black guy had moved closer to them. He emitted a sound that was somewhere between clearing his throat and a growl.

A voice floated out of a speaker on the blonde's desk, "Bring them in, Samantha. I'll be happy to talk to them." Krystal glanced at the CCTV camera on the wall behind the receptionist. Wakefield had been watching them and apparently could hear them, too.

"Follow me." Samantha led them down the main corridor to a pair of polished wood doors at the end. She knocked softly and ushered them into George Wakefield's presence.

The office was large and paneled with some sort of exotic shiny wood. A lot of the wall space was occupied by an extensive collection of photographs of Wakefield with dozens of Washington personalities and politicians, including a couple of presidents – the omnipresent Washington, D.C. vanity wall. There were a lot of photos of bearded men in uniform in what might have been somewhere in Latin America, Afghanistan or Iraq and several of Wakefield posing in various native garb. Deeply stuffed leather chairs were gathered around a large coffee table. A well-stocked wet bar stretched along one wall, and a bookcase along another.

Krystal studied the man who rose from behind a large, ornate mahogany desk. He had to be over sixty and was of medium height and stocky. His white neatly cut hair was carefully parted and contrasted sharply with his tanned face. The suit, she thought, was too showy. It was made of a shiny, brown fabric with wide, light blue pinstripes, and a light blue silk handkerchief peeked from the breast pocket to match the tie. The word that sprang immediately to mind was dapper, but after a moment that changed. He could just as easily be a guy at home wearing a polyester Hawaiian shirt with a gold chain around his neck in Miami Beach. He gave mixed signals.

Wakefield's face creased in a smile to display small, evenly spaced white teeth. "Welcome. Let's all sit over around the table."

The receptionist hovered by the door, and he said, "Samantha, why don't you bring us some coffee." He gave a solicitous look at Krystal and Watson. "Or would you prefer something else, coke, Sprite?"

"No, thanks," said Krystal. "We just have a few questions, and then we'll be going."

Wakefield raised an inquisitve eyebrow and waved the receptionist away. "OK," he said, "shoot. How can I help you? I see from your badges that you're from the Arlington Police."

Wakefield's face, dominated by a prominent Roman nose, was open and inviting as he waited for Krystal to speak, the kind of expression used to feign innocence.

She introduced herself and Watson, who seemed to like her giving him the title of detective. "We're investigating the murder of Dugan Dillon. We understand he was your firm's lawyer and were hoping you could tell us something about him." Watson pulled out a notebook and pen.

Wakefield studied them for beat. His expression remained friendly, but his green eyes turned a darker shade. "If I recall correctly," he said, "that murder took place a couple of months ago over in your bailiwick. It was all over the news for a while."

"That's right," she said. The man had not answered the question. "Was he your firm's attorney?"

"Well," he said, "that might not be entirely accurate. Did he do some legal work for us? Yes, he occasionally handled minor contractual matters over the past couple of years, but he was not our corporate attorney."

"May I ask who is your corporate attorney?"

"Well, it's no secret. Paul Dillon handles most of our legal affairs."

"Can you think of any reason Dugan might have been killed?"

Wakefield knitted his brows. "Why would you ask me such a thing?"

"There was nothing connected to his work for you that might have served as a motive?"

He stared straight at her, the image of virtue. "Not a thing."

"Anything, even something that seems unimportant, could help," she persisted. "Are you absolutely certain?"

"Detective," he said, "I've spent a lifetime looking at complicated problems and coming up with solutions, and I'm damned good at it. When I say there's nothing, I mean it."

He rose to indicate the meeting was over. "Now, if there's nothing else ..."

Krystal and Watson exchanged a glance and stood. Wakefield escorted them back to the reception area where they shook hands all around. The big black guy stared at them from a chair near the doors.

"Thanks for your time, Mr. Wakefield," said

Krystal. "We'll call if there are any more questions."

"You do that," said Wakefield. "Next time, please call first."

Back on the sidewalk, she asked, "What did you think?"

"I think he's a shifty bastard in a shiny suit. Looks like a used car salesman."

"But we did confirm that the Dillons worked for him."

"Yeah, for all the good it does. He sure as hell didn't tell us anything else."

"It's more than we knew before, and it partially confirms Apelbaum's story. I wonder if I should have asked about the Russians. You know, the stuff in the article. But I just think it's too early. I want to find out a few more facts before going there. We can always come back again."

They started back for the car, but Krystal stopped before they'd walked very far and pulled out her cell phone. She had an idea. There was someone near-by who might be able to tell them a lot more about George Wakefield.

"Who're you calling?" asked Watson.

"A friend of mine. He has an office here on 'K' Street."

"Pretty high cotton around here," he observed.

CHAPTER 9

Robert Strachey was restless. His current portfolio at his uncle's lobbying firm was to protect the interests of tomato importers, including the biggest chains of supermarkets in the country. The pledge of one of the presidential candidates to initiate protectionist import tariffs had his clients worried. When his car phone rang he was on his way back to his office following a series of meetings with members of Congress, each and every one of which would be happy to look after the interests of foreign tomato growers for a generous contribution to their campaign war chests. By mid-morning Strachey had lost the ability to genuflect and smile like 1930's actor Stepin Fetchit. "Fetchit," actually a man named Lincoln Theodore Monroe Andrew Perry, was the first black movie actor to become a millionaire. But Strachey was no good at shucking and jiving, even for big money, and on the best of days had little use for politicians, a definite drawback in his current job.

Strachey used to be an intelligence officer, a CIA Clandestine Services star, before circumstances and his own conscience made it impossible to continue. The theory is that once an intelligence officer, always an intelligence officer did not mean that links to the Agency never were severed. No, it meant that the traits ingrained into such people, their experiences, special knowledge, and instincts did not vanish when they left. Sometimes, for such people, normal life could be restrictive, like a suit that was ever so slightly too small.

Strachey still tended to check for surveillance every time he sat in a car or took a walk and note the locations of possible dead drop sites. He didn't know if he did this for amusement or because he couldn't help himself. What he did know was that he struggled daily with boredom despite the obscene amount of money he made as a lobbyist. Tomatoes were no substitute for espionage.

The call from his friend, Krystal Murphy, offered a welcome respite. She said she was on 'K' Street and wondered if she could drop by his office. It was nearing one P.M., so he suggested they meet for lunch instead. It would delay his return to the office.

He told her to meet him at the Four Seasons Hotel in Georgetown and altered his course toward 'M' Street.

In the car with Krystal, Watson said, "The Four Seasons? Now that's getting into some really high cotton. I hope your rich friend is paying."

She laughed, "Oh, he always pays. He's a good guy, and I've sort of worked with him a couple of times. He was a spook before he moved to 'K' Street."

"Well, hell," said Watson, "he moved from one den of coyotes to another. Gives me all sorts of confidence."

"Don't be like that. You'll see. He's a good guy, and he hates his job."

"Then why does he stay?"

She rubbed her thumb and forefinger together, "Why do you think?"

They found Strachey waiting at a table in the restaurant at the rear of the Four Seasons lobby. He rose as they approached. The former spook was shorter than Watson by a few inches, had brown hair graying at the temples, and wore an expensive suit that draped well over an athletic frame. Watson guessed his age at near fifty.

Introductions over and orders given, Krystal asked, "What do you know about a guy named George Wakefield?"

"That's a name to conjure with," said Strachey. "He's a legend at Langley, at least among the old boys that are left. Depending on who's talking, he's either a daring operational genius or an absolute asshole. There isn't anything in between. He was what we used to call a cowboy, ready to go in with guns blazing without too much thinking about consequences beforehand. Why do you ask?"

Krystal gave him the background on their investigation, Apelbaum's article, and the recent double murder.

"Russians, eh," he said, "George didn't have a lot to do with the Russians in the old days, except maybe in Afghanistan – but then it was long distance and via the Mujihadeen. He spent a lot of time in Latin America corrupting officials and overthrowing their governments. And he favored loud clothes. I used to think his tailor must be Barnum and Bailey. But don't let all that fool you. He was damned effective at what he did, and to his credit he didn't care who he pissed off. He was a high-roller, and he made it to the top by sheer force of will."

Krystal thought back to the dapper older man they'd just met, and Strachey's description fit. There was a hard man behind the showy veneer.

"But you don't remember him having a lot to do

with the Russians?" asked Watson.

"Well," said Strachey, "back in the day when the Soviets were the number one target, everybody had something to do with them wherever they were. I guess George must have had his share, and when he reached the top ranks it would have been inevitable."

"Why did he leave the CIA?" she asked.

"Mutual dislike, I guess. He was just too scandal prone for some of the new guys. He was part of an old guard which represented too many skeletons in the closet."

"What have you heard about what he's doing now?" asked Krystal.

"I haven't seen him in years, but I know he started some sort of consulting company in D.C. and was still poking his finger in peoples' eyes."

"What do you think about the stuff Apelbaum wrote?"

"Dirty tricks on politicians?" Strachey couldn't suppress a chuckle. "That'd be right up George's alley. But working with the Russians to influence U.S. elections? I dunno. That would be a bridge too far, even for a guy like George."

"Can you see him having any sort of contact with Russian Intelligence?"

"Well, that's not so hard these days, is it? It's not like it was before with the Soviets. George has a lot of old spooks working for him, and Russian contacts can be useful in the kind of work he does. He works internationally, you know."

"Could he be doing anything worth killing to hide?"

Strachey had ordered a bottle of Pauillac for

them to share, and he didn't speak as he topped up glasses all around. He set the bottle down and said, "Murder and Russians go hand in glove these days. I suppose that if George hasn't been careful he could have gotten himself mixed up with some bad hombres."

"And from what you say, he's not a particularly careful guy. I don't suppose you could check it out," said Krystal.

"Me?"

"This town is filled with old spooks. They crop up everywhere, like mushrooms. There might be some information floating around the rumor circuit. You'd be doing me a big favor."

He took a sip of his wine. "And in return you could get me out of some speeding tickets?" He grinned. "Might be fun to do a little sleuthing. Nobody likes to tell tales more than old spies, and a lot of them hate one another.   I can dig around at the Metropolitan Club and Cosmos, and I know some other fellows I can trust to be discreet."

Watson interjected. "Whoa, slow down! You might be right, Krystal, but all we have to go on is a story from an anoynmous source, a really anonymous source. We don't know for sure if Wakefield's involved, but it's only fair to warn Bob here that three people have already been killed. I ain't so sure about getting a civilian involved."

"I can take care of myself," said Strachey.

Watson rolled his eyes.

"Frank," said Krystal, "believe me, Bob can take care of himself."

"Don't worry, Frank," said Strachey. "To quote

my favorite song, 'A Country Boy Can Survive.'"

Watson looked unconvinced, but he was impressed that someone like Strachey would know the Hank Williams, Jr. song.

Strachey gave him an easy grin. "Frank, you're an old Georgia boy, so take it from an old North Carolina boy that he knows what he's talking about. I've spent as much time in the woods as you."

Watson was startled when Strachey's voice took on the sweet Carolinian intonations. "Well, I'll be damned. My mama always told me never to miss a good chance to shut up."

Krystal laughed out loud and raised her wine glass in a toast. "To country boys," she said. For the first time since she'd seen Dugan Dillon's body, she felt a surge of hope.

CHAPTER 10

A tall, thin man with a sallow face, shaved skull, and glacial blue eyes pushed through the door into George Wakefield's office. His name was Yuriy, he was in his mid-fifties, and he walked with a limp.

Wakefield did not particularly care for Yuriy, nor did he trust him completely. The Russian resided in the Brighton Beach section of Brooklyn where he was ostensibly employed by a dry cleaner whose premises he had never entered. His real employer was a very wealthy man in Moscow and a former KGB officer.

He was in fact one of several illegal operatives the man and his FSB friends had planted across the United States, and he had but one job – eliminating targets designated by his master.

Wakefield waved him to a chair while he paced around the room. "We might have a problem."

The Russian's face remained impassive. "What do you mean?"

"I was just visited by two police officers about the Dugan Dillon thing." He avoided the word 'murder' because it made even him queasy, something to which he was unaccustomed.

"Yes?" Yuriy's cold eyes bored into the American. "What did they want with you?"

"They asked if Dugan worked for me. We've been careful to avoid anything getting out, but it must have been that damned story on the Internet, unless Paul Dillon's said something. And he wouldn't. He knows better, and so does Dugan's wife."

"I was about to return to Brighton Beach," said Yuriy. He'd completed his latest task the night before and was ready to sink back into the anonymity provided by the seedy Russian enclave in Brooklyn. "Should I stay?"

"Maybe. I haven't decided. They didn't mention Russia."

"But ... ?"

"But I'm sure the story brought them here, and the story mentioned Russia. They'll start sniffing around now, you can bet on it. I'm not sure what we can do."

"Should I ask for instructions?"

"Hell no! Moscow can't do anything about it. We'll wait and see what develops. I was thinking about tracking the cops."

Yuriy drew himself up. "I was trained by the best. No one will see me."

Wakefield turned on him with some heat. "I was trained by the best, too, Yuriy, and I know that one man can't run a surveillance without being spotted sooner or later. The cops aren't blind or stupid. No, you go back to Brooklyn for the time being. My own people can handle this."

"Moscow will not be pleased. This was supposed to be a simple elimination, but it's getting complicated. I told you that two more killings would cause a problem."

Wakefield half muttered to himself. "I can put some discreet feelers out. Go on back to Brighton Beach until you hear from me. If more wet work is called for, I'll contact you."

Wakefield watched Yuriy limp out of the room.

The limp, he knew, was from a Mujihadeen bullet in Aghanistan.

For now, he'd bide his time, put an ear to the old boy network and hope there were no negative vibrations. The most immediate item on his agenda was to warn Paul Dillon that he might be questioned. He'd already made sure the high-priced lawyer would keep his mouth shut.

CHAPTER 11

"Let's go back to the office and scour the Internet for information on Wakefield. With that guy's background, we're sure to turn up something."

They were on the way back to Arlington Police HQS. Watson replied, "You've got the bit between your teeth now, don't you?"

"To put it in terms you might understand, Frank, so far we've been drilling a dry hole, but now something is beginning to bubble up."

"Er, sure, Red. It's bubbling alright." Watson shook his head.

By the end of the day they'd read a lot about George Wakefield. Most of the press accounts were negative, especially as concerned the man's long record of activities in Latin America. Overall, Robert Strachey's description was supported by what they saw. But there wasn't a whisper of any connection between Wakefield and Russia.

Krystal leaned away from the computer screen and rubbed her eyes with the backs of her hands. "Well, shit," she said.

"We know a helluva lot more about Wakefield now than we did this morning," said Watson, "We should have done this first – done more thorough research before talking to the man."

"I thought of that," said Krystal, "but sometimes that approach leads to preconceptions and shuts down your receptivity to first impressions. And we had to get to him as soon as possible after the Alexandria murders."

"That's a pretty interesting approach, Red, really counter-intuitive."

"That's a big word for a country boy, Frank," she smiled.

"Well, the one-eyed hog and all that, you know."

"Uh, huh, right." There was no doubting Watson's intelligence. He liked to hide it behind a folksy exterior, but he was sharp. Also, he didn't treat her differently because of her sex and did not resent her rise in the ranks.

"We'll go see Paul Dillon first thing tomorrow," she said. "Go home to your wife and kids and relax."

After Watson left she scanned the Internet material on Wakefield one more time before calling it a day herself. She wasn't in a hurry to go home. There was no one waiting for her there, no family, not even a cat. And she knew the first thing she'd do was pour a stiff scotch. She'd weaned herself from the single malts to the cheaper blends because a new bottle every three or four days was becoming expensive.

She could put this day in the plus column. Maybe it would help her sleep a little better. She just hoped she could build some momentum in the case. After two months, they finally had a new trail to follow but it was still first steps.

"Did you notice?" asked Krystal.

"What?"

"That he used the same words as George Wakefield – '... he handled a couple of minor contractual matters' for Wakefield, but nothing more. He wants us to think Dugan's connection to Wakefield was peripheral, at most."

"Maybe it was."

"And he definitely did not want to say anything more about Wakefield and his outfit."

"Attorney – client privilege."

Krystal snorted her disgust. She and Watson were on the way back to the office after their second meeting with Paul Dillon. Their reception had been decidedly frosty, and Dillon had answered their questions with studied conciseness.

"Did you notice his reaction when we asked about the Russians?"

Watson wrinkled his nose. "He went stone cold. Yep, I'd say it got a rise out of him."

"Christ, Frank, we're talking about the cold-blooded murder of his own son. He should be falling all over himself to help us."

"You think?"

"We're running out of people to talk to. Everyone involved is stonewalling, and there's not a damned thing we can do about it."

"Maybe your ex-CIA buddy will come up with something."

"It's a longshot."

"It is, but we might flush something out of the bushes."

CHAPTER 12

Robert Strachey was having fun. In the week since Krystal Murphy asked for his help, he'd renewed old acquaintances around town. To his surprise, mixing with people from his old tribe was somehow invigorating. For the most part he'd avoided contact with the Agency and his fellow alumni since resigning. But he had to admit it was pleasant to talk with people with whom he shared common experiences and thought patterns.

There is a plethora of former CIA officers salted in various private companies around Washington these days or working independently. Too many of them spent only a few years in the Agency, just enough time to take advantage of the quarter of a million dollars the government lavished on them for training and security clearances. They are permitted to keep their clearances and advertise themselves as "former intelligence officers." It makes for a nice résumé entry in a town that gobbles up people with expensive security clearances already in place. Résumé enhancement is not the ideal motivation for becoming an intelligence officer. Older model spooks completed their thirty years and gratefully retired to more peaceful pursuits and welcomed anonymity.

On this day in late summer, Strachey steered his BMW past the Kennedy Center and across the George Washington Bridge where he took the down ramp onto the George Washington Parkway affording a scenic drive northwest along the Potomac past the Three Sisters islands. The Rt. 123 exit led him past the entrance to CIA toward McLean, but he did not follow his regular route to the house on Meadowbrook Avenue that he shared with his wife, Amy, their son, R.T., and his father-in-law, the cantankerous Thomas Jefferson Dawson. The fact that the latter was now nearing 90 years-old had neither slowed him appreciably nor cured him of the habit of stating his mind.

Instead Strachey continued west until he encountered Tyson's Corner, where he pulled into the parking garage of the Ritz-Carlton Hotel. He took the elevator from the garage up to the spacious bar and scanned the room until he found the face he was looking for. Harvey Grant was staring straight at him and raised his arm to beckon him to a seat. He'd chosen a quiet corner to the left of the bar.

Grant, a former chief of the CIA's analytical division, the DDI, had been elevated to Deputy Director of the CIA in the previous administration. How a man of such rectitude and common sense had maintained his position through the recent years of politicization of the Agency, Strachey could not fathom. Harvey Grant was "old school," a condition unwelcome at the top of the reorganized Agency.

"Take a seat," said Grant, indicating an overstuffed leather chair. "I already told the waiter you would want a nice single malt. I ordered an Oban for you."

"Thanks," answered Strachey. He could use a drink.

He studied his old friend as the waiter delivered his drink along with a little bowl of mixed nuts. Grant had always seemed "old" to him, but now there was also a hint of incipient fragility about the man. His movements were careful and slow. He guided his hand as he reached for his glass of white wine with as much care as if he were landing a jet on an aircraft carrier.

"Do you ever think about going back, Robert?" There was a gleam in Grant's eyes as he said this.

"No." Strachey's reply was firm and fast. "I cut the cord a long time ago, and you know the reason why."

Grant closed his eyes and nodded slowly. Strachey had killed a man, assassinated him in cold blood with a Russian sniper rifle. The man, a defector, had been in CIA custody at the time, but he was responsible for the death of Strachey's mentor, and that could not be forgiven. Barely a handful of people knew it had been Strachey's doing, but his conscience would not permit him to remain in the Agency after betraying it.

The older man sighed. "You, know, Robert, it's probably just as well. It's no longer the Agency you knew, and the people who run it no longer have very much in common with you. There have been many changes, and not all of them for the better."

Strachey sipped his Oban. "So I hear." His wife, Amy, was still one of the top computer analysts at Langley.

Grant shook his head in silent acquiescence. "So, to what do I owe the pleasure of this reunion?"

"I'm doing a favor for Krystal."

Grant perked up at the mention of Murphy. "She's done well for herself, hasn't she? No one deserves it more. What kind of favor?"

Michael R. Davidson

"She's interested in George Wakefield."

"Oh, my Lord. Has he finally done something he can be arrested for?"

"I don't know. Krystal is working on a murder, and George popped up on her radar. She's trying to find out what he's been up to and whether he has anything to do with the Russians."

"Ah, the Dillon murder, I would guess." Grant closed his eyes again. "What's the connection?" His voice dropped an octave. *Was that wariness in his voice?*

"She doesn't know. It's just another line of inquiry based on something that appeared on a cheesy website."

"I don't know if I can be of any help, Bob."

The way he said it could have meant anything. Either Grant had no pertinent information, or he knew something, but it was classified. "Does that mean you know nothing or that you couldn't tell me if you did?"

"Yes."

Sometimes an affirmative answer is the most ambiguous answer. Strachey chuckled, "I'm not a Congressional committee, Harvey."

"How important is this to you?" Grant regarded him with serious eyes over the tops of his wire-rimmed spectacles.

"It might help solve a murder."

"That's not necessarily a criterion the CIA would accept, you know."

"I know." What was important to the CIA was the protection of secrets, sources, and methods, a philosophy directly opposed to that of the press and sometimes the cops. "So, there's nothing you can tell me?"

Grant took a careful sip of wine. He answered with a question. "You haven't asked Amy to get involved in this, have you?"

"No."

"Don't. It could be dangerous."

This was startling. "Dangerous, how?"

"Very," said Grant staring him straight in the eye. "And if it gets around that you're taking an interest, it could be dangerous for you, too. It might be best if you just let the police handle it."

"I've already talked to some old hands."

"Did you find out anything?"

"No. Most people just shake their heads where George is concerned."

"Does Krystal still have her contact at the FBI?"

"I suppose so."

"She might find some help there."

Harvey Grant wasn't going to say more, and this was troubling but maybe understandable. In fact, it spoke volumes. "OK, Harvey. I understand. No hard feelings."

"Remember what I said, Bob. And if you've been poking around, please keep an eye over your shoulder." Grant was deadly serious.

"I will."

Yes, there was definitely something to the idea that Wakefield was involved in some way with the Russians, and the CIA knew about it. "Poking around" could be dangerous. Three dead men already attested to that. The favor he was doing for Krystal Murphy suddenly turned several shades darker.

CHAPTER 13

The car parked across the street when Strachey turned into his driveway on Meadowbrook Avenue did not escape his notice. It was not a car he recognized as belonging to one of his neighbors. A man was in the driver's seat.

He mentally filed the car and D.C. license number. This was an old habit from his days in the field, something he did automatically whenever something seemed out of place. But the presence of a strange car in the neighborhood was not particularly alarming or even unusual. When he looked out a window fifteen minutes later, it was gone.

The more he thought about the conversation with Harvey Grant the more it troubled him. Harvey knew something. The mention of a possible connection between the Russians and George Wakefield had stimulated a definite response. He had a long and close friendship with the senior CIA official, and it was unlike him to hold back.

He decided to follow Harvey's advice not to raise the subject with Amy, at least not yet.

Krystal was hung over. A light dinner of cold chicken and a salad followed by three scotches combined to give her a restless night and a morning headache. She swallowed a couple of aspirin along with three glasses of water, counting on rehydration to eliminate the dryness in her mouth and the pounding in her temples. She felt only slightly better by the time she stepped into her office carrying a large Starbucks cup filled with black coffee.

She'd barely had time to scan the morning reports before Watson rapped lightly on the door frame and slouched into a chair in front of her desk. "Morning, Red," he said.

"Umph," she grunted.

Watson cocked his head and peered at her. "You OK, Red? You look a little peaked this morning." He pronounced it "pikud," meaning pale and slightly under the weather.

Krystal held back the snarl that rose in her throat and amended it to a mumbled, "I'm OK. It's just a headache." In the mirror that morning her eyes had betrayed a weariness that could not be concealed.

"Erm, OK. What are we doing today?"

Her brain was still too numb to think. She promised herself to lay off the scotch tonight. "What do you think we should do, Frank?"

"We could dig a little deeper into Paul Dillon's contacts, maybe interview one or two of them."

"And word of that would get back to Dillon immediately."

"Yeah, he'd probably raise a shit storm. But maybe stirring things up would be a good thing. You never know what might jump out of the bushes."

It wouldn't be the first time Krystal had faced push-back in an investigation. It was never a pleasant experience, and she wasn't ready to increase the odds against her just yet. Dillon's old boy network would instinctively protect one of their own.

"Let's go over the info on Wakefield's outfit again. We might get farther there, and Bob's inquiries might come up with something. George Wakefield is not the most beloved man in Washington."

It was the same car. It had picked Strachey up on Chain Bridge Road as he left home for the office and was now three cars behind him in the rush hour traffic on Dolly Madison Boulevard.

He decided to follow his normal route into the city to his office. He'd spend the morning there and then go to a late luncheon appointment at The Prime Rib. It was only a few blocks away on 'K' Street, but he would make a few stops on the way.

He made the guy by the second stop when he ducked into a stationery shop. There was only the one surveillant. He was tall and thin and dressed in black like a 1990's Moscow hood. He loitered in plain sight on the sidewalk outside the shop.

Either the guy was a lousy surveillant or he didn't care if he was spotted. Maybe this was intended as a warning.

Strachey paused at the restaurant entrance and turned to watch the man in black walk past. He had a long, sallow face and slightly slanted eyes that were close together under shaggy brows. He looked straight at Strachey and gave him a ghastly smile before disappearing into the noon-day crowd on the sidewalk. He walked with a limp.

Krystal knocked on the door of the house on Meadowbrook Avenue, and it was opened immediately by a petite woman with *café au lait* skin and large green eyes. This was Amy Strachey, and her face creased with a welcoming smile as she embraced Krystal.

"Come on in. It's been way too long since we've seen you in this house." She stood back and surveyed Krystal who had come straight from the office and was still dressed in her usual jeans and polo shirt. She'd hesitated to accept the invitation, but Bob Strachey had been insistent on the phone.

Waiting to greet her was Amy's father, Thomas Jefferson Dawson, an elderly very black man with closely cropped white hair and a twinkle in his eye. Thomas was irrascible with nearly everyone else, but he had a soft spot for the auburn haired detective. Clinging to his side was "R.T.", Bob and Amy's year old son. "Take a look at this big boy," said Thomas, "he's growing like a weed, ain't he?"

The last time she'd seen R.T. he was little more than a babe in arms. The boy gave her a bold look and a big smile. "Hi, R.T.," she said, "I brought you a present." She'd stopped on the way to pick up a teddy bear that was about half R.T.'s size."

"Daddy," said Amy, "why don't you put R.T. in his playpen with his new bear. Dinner's about ready." She disappeared into the kitchen, and Thomas headed for the nursery.

Bob waited until they were out of the room to whisper, "Somebody's following me, and I don't think it's a coincidence that it began after I started asking questions about Wakefield. Did you see anything before coming in?"

"No. Did they follow you home?"

"No. They were outside the house last night, and behind me on the way into the city this morning. Then again when I walked to lunch. Funny thing is, they weren't particularly careful about it. I think they wanted me to see them."

"A warning?"

"Seems like. I didn't like the guy's looks. I'm worried, given that it's a murder investigation. I don't like to think I've put my family in danger."

Krystal felt a pang of remorse. "Have you told Amy?"

"No, Harvey Grant told me not to, but I just don't see how I can avoid it now because my wife won't take precautions unless she knows the reason. I'm going to suggest that Thomas and Amy take R.T. for a long visit to Charolotte." Amy had been raised by her father in North Carolina.

A huge wave of guilt washed over Krystal. She'd had no business asking a civilian for help, even if Strachey did know how to take care of himself.

Reading her thoughts, he said, "Don't worry. I don't blame you. To tell the truth, I welcomed the chance to do something interesting for a change."

"I should never have asked you, Bob. I don't know what to say. I'd never forgive myself if anything happened to you or Amy."

"Like I said, it looked like a warning. I didn't see anything on the way home. But I'll keep an eye out, and you should watch your six, too."

"What are you two whispering about?" Amy had begun to lay the table.

Strachey shot a guilty look over his shoulder. "Just business," he said.

Amy eyed them both with a mixture of suspicion and amusement. "Again? What are you two mixed up in now? Fess up."

"Let's talk about it after dinner," said Strachey. "After Thomas and R.T. have gone to bed.

"So it's serious?"

"It's beginning to look like it."

After the meal Amy put R.T. to bed, and Thomas excused himself to go to his room where he would watch re-runs of old TV shows. He'd become addicted to cable TV.

The three of them retired to the living room where Amy served drinks before taking a seat from which she eyed them curiously. "Well, spill it. You hardly spoke at all during dinner."

Strachey turned to Krystal. "Are you sure it's OK for me to talk about your case?"

"In for a penny ... ," she replied. "As Watson might say, the barn door's already open." She turned to Amy. "I'm sorry, Amy. I shouldn't have asked Bob to get involved."

Now Amy was seriously worried and waited for her husband to speak.

"Krystal has been working on the Dugan Dillon murder case for a couple of months," he began.

When he was finished Amy shook her head in disbelief. "And you say Harvey Grant warned you not to talk to me about this?"

"Yep. Other than that, he was tight-lipped. I assumed I'd stumbled into classified territory, but his reaction was strange."

Amy knit her brow in concentration. "I can't think of anything. Nothing related has come across my screen. If it's a classified Agency matter, it's way above my pay grade or it's a highly compartentalized case. Harvey is now Number Two at Langley and breathing rarified Seventh Floor air every day. I don't see him as often as I used to. But I can't believe he'd leave you hanging if he thought you were in some kind of danger."

"I agree. Harvey's one of the good guys."

"One of the few good guys left on the Seventh Floor," said Amy. "The place has become very politicized. Our job is to steal secrets and remain objective, not support one Washington faction against another. RUMINT says the DCI is leaking stuff to the press."

"RUMINT?" The term was unfamiliar to Krystal.

Amy giggled. "Rumor intelligence, chatter in the hallways."

But Strachey remained serious. "I want you and R.T. and Thomas to get out of town for awhile. Take a vacation to North Carolina, visit some relatives. My folks would be thrilled to have you for awhile up in Asheville."

"You want me to run away?" She was indignant.

"In a word, yes," said Strachey. "I know you can take care of yourself, but we have to think of your father and R.T. I don't want them stuck in the middle of something that could turn nasty in a hurry."

Still unconvinced, Amy said, "And what about you? What will you do while we're away?"

"That's a fair question," he replied. "And to be frank, I'm not sure. All I've done is contact some old boys and ask about Wakefield's activities. You know how the old boy gossip network functions. They have lines into everything. There's no solid evidence, but a good guess would be that word of my inquiries got back to Wakefield, and the surveillance is the result. I want to see where this leads. Maybe that's the end of it. But I want freedom of action if it's not."

"Meaning you want us out of the way," said Amy.

"Meaning I want to protect my family."

"Why didn't you tell me about this before?" Amy shot an accusatory glance at Krystal who had remained silent throughout.

"Frankly, I never imagined it would come to anything like this," said Strachey. "It seemed a bit of harmless fun shooting the shit with the old boys."

"Maybe I could dig something up at Langley."

"I don't think that's a good idea. Remember how adamant Harvey was that I not involve you. And if your networks haven't shown you anything by now, you'd only be running the chance that the Seventh Floor will come down on you hard."

"I see your point," said Amy. "What do you think, Krystal? Is this thing really so dangerous?"

The entire conversation between her friends was deeply embarrassing to Krystal. They would not be facing this problem had she not thoughtlessly asked Strachey to do her a favor. Bringing civilians into a case was not something cops should do. Frank Watson had been skeptical of the tactic, and he'd been right.

"Don't blame Bob, Amy. This is all my fault, and I'm sorry. I was at a dead end in the investigation, and when Wakefield popped up, a former CIA guy, my first thought was to turn to Bob. I was looking for a shortcut, and should never have done it. I think Bob should just drop it now so you can get on with your lives."

Amy looked hopefully at her husband.

"I'm not so sure," he said. "Until we can be sure there's no hostile intent, I still like the vacation idea. If it's all clear after a couple of weeks, we can all get back to normal."

Amy looked defeated, and it made Krystal feel all the worse. But Strachey's desire to be free of distractions for the time being was sound. And knowing her friend, she didn't think Strachey was about to leave the field.

CHAPTER 14

It was after ten when she returned to the North Barton Street apartment. She needed a drink, badly. Her conscience was in overdrive. Bringing Strachey into the case had been a mistake, but now he had the bit between his teeth and refused to be called off. In fact, he seemed to relish the experience, especially since his decision to move his family to a safe distance. Krystal suspected Robert regretted leaving the Agency, missed the work. He never spoke about it, though, and she had no idea why he had resigned when he was apparently at the top of his game. The death of his friend and mentor Terrance Stoddard had affected him deeply. Of that there could be no doubt.

She switched on the television and fell onto the couch with a second scotch. She woke up in the same position in the morning with a mouth filled with cotton and a headache.

A loud clap of thunder drew her attention to the windows. The noise must have been what woke her up. A summer storm was driving a hard rain onto Arlington, and the sky was darkening to match her mood. What the hell was the matter with her? She'd worked hard, had a successful career, and was recognized for her work. But satisfaction had become elusive.

Was it the fabled biological clock ticking away somewhere deep inside that made her so restless? She was edging closer to forty than to thirty. Was it so important? She had an on-going relationship with a wonderful man, but that man was a thousand miles away and showing signs of dissatisfaction with the arrangement.

No matter how hard she worked, how many successes she had, there was an undercurrent of melancholy, a sort of leitmotif to her life that she had only recently begun to notice. The Irish were moody folk, given to strong emotions, but she felt emotionally flat except for the times she and Ray Velazquez were together. There was a message in all this. An elastic band inside her was stretching to its breaking point.

She surveyed her small apartment, the best she could afford on a cop's salary. It was furnished with an eclectic assortment of furniture she'd managed to collect over the years with no particular style in mind. The table at the end of the couch held a lamp and a framed photograph of her as a pigtailed Hoosier teenager with her arms around Ozzie, the family German Shepherd. There was a bookcase that still held her college criminology texts, an assortment of old family photos, and the miniature cow collection she'd started while still in grade school. In the bedroom there were more photos of her family, and a snapshot of Ray Velazquez was on the refrigerator door, held there by a magnet. But all of these people, her family and Ray, were far away.

She'd been desperate to escape the flat fields of her childhood along the Wabash. Life there had seemed so bland. The small towns and cities had declined with the closing of the coal mines. Terre Haute was now but a shabby shell of its former self. But her brother, his wife and children who still maintained the family farm seemed content and happy. They led simple lives and were satisfied with simple things. They were normal people, unlike her.

Alone in an apartment that offered nothing to lift her spirits, with the storm raging outside beating down the trees in the park across the street, she was overcome by a sense of desolation and a sudden rush of unfamiliar self-pity. This was the life she had made for herself. Real friends she could count on the fingers of one hand. Roberty Strachey and his wife, Amy, and Frank Watson's family. And Ray Velazquez who seemed to be slipping away.

In the Army, although the Military Police were not everybody's favorites, she'd enjoyed the camaraderie of her fellow soldiers. A very attractive girl, she'd been popular in college, which she'd attended thanks to the G.I. Bill. Week-ends had rarely found her without a date or without a group of fun-loving friends. But her life entered an entirely different phase when she became a police officer and applied herself single-mindedly to building a career. In the process she had somehow isolated herself.

She showered and held her face under the spray for a long time to wash away the unexpected tears.

By the time she made it into the office she felt as though she had the weight of the world on her shoulders and apparently looked it, too, judging from Frank Watson's concerned expression.

"Are you OK, Red? You look like somebody killed your dog."

"That bad, huh?"

"'Fraid so. Let me get you a cup of coffee."

She held up her Starbucks cup and waved it in front of him.

He gave her a dubious look. "I don't think that'll be enough. I'm gonna brew a fresh pot."

He left as Krystal drained the last dregs from the paper cup and tossed it into a wastebasket. She tried to piece together what they had so far. First, the dead lawyer, then the blog article, the interview with Wakefield, two more deaths, and now Strachey's strange pursuer. And every trail they followed crashed against a stone wall.

Watson returned with two steaming mugs of black coffee and thrust one in front of her.

"This case getting you down, Red?" He studied her over the rim of his mug.

"We have nothing but victims and questions, Frank. And after two months that's not nearly enough. And I'm getting squawks to get you back in uniform."

"I'm beginning to like this soft life you detectives lead." He pronounced it DEE-tectives. "Maybe I'll put in my papers to transfer in here permanently."

"Christ, Frank, you should have seen enough already to make you nostalgic for uniforms and donuts."

He laughed. "Maybe you should try it, Red. You were pretty good when you wore the uniform."

"Which one, battle dress or blue?"

"Oh, both, I'm sure. I ain't suggesting you re-enlist."

"It was a simpler life."

"Well," he said, "I surely don't miss Iraq. Not one sweet bit."

That elicited a weak smile. "Me neither, Frank, me neither."

"Damn camel jockeys. I never saw a place more fucked up."

"FUBAR," she agreed. "But I never saw a camel over there."

"Well," he said, "now that we got that out of the way, what are we gonna do next.?"

She had to admit it: Frank Watson could pull her out of a foul mood like no one else in Arlington. What was it about Southern men?

She told him about the evening with the Stracheys. "I'm sure Bob will be out there beating the bushes today. But it still worries me."

"I dunno, Red, you sure he can take care of himself."

"Yeah," she said, "I'm pretty sure he's ignoring D.C. law and carrying a piece into the District today."

"A spook with a piece? Somehow that doesn't seem like a good idea."

"You haven't see him shoot. He saved my ass once."

Watson gave her a dubious look, thinking of the Washington lobbyist in the two thousand dollar suit he'd met at the Four Seasons. "No shit?"

"It was awhile ago, but take my word for it. Bob Strachey is a badass."

"OK, the old spook is a badass. But so is whoever is popping these guys off."

The phone on Krystal's desk rang. She picked up, listened, and gave Watson a strangled look. "It's the Chief," she said, "He wants to see me."

"Shit." He pronounced it SHEE-it with two distinct syllables.

Fifteen minutes later, Krystal stepped into the

Chief's office. Heck peered curiously at her from behind his desk. "Are you feeling alright, Murphy? If you don't mind my saying, you don't look well."

"I'm OK, Chief." She was embarrassed that Heck confirmed Watson's observation.

"I hope so." He frowned. "You need to take better care of yourself. Take a seat, please."

She sat and imagined that she must look like something the cat dragged in.

Heck studied her for a beat longer and said, "I've been receiving phone calls from Paul Dillon and a couple of his friends, friends who seem to believe they have a lot of influence in the county. They complain that you're harassing the Dillon family. What do you have to say about that?"

Krystal felt her "Irish" rising and tamped it down. "Harrassment? All we've done is follow wherever the leads, the very few leads, take us. We did pay a second visit to Dillon's office to ask about Dugan's connection to George Wakefield, but he told us nothing. I just can't understand why he's not being more forthcoming with us about the murder of his own son. It doesn't make sense. There's something about the Wakefield connection that no one wants to talk about, especially when we ask about Russians. After two months the only two people who might know anything, according to the 'All the Truth' piece. No, I wouldn't call asking the vic's father for help harassment."

"Well," said Heck, "neither would I, and I don't like even a hint of political pressure on a police investigation. So don't worry. I've got your back. I just wanted you to know about the calls. I agree, it's odd."

Her first reaction was surprise. When Heck had mentioned the complaints she'd been ready for a dressing down. She'd become accustomed to former Chief Fogerty's preoccupation with keeping his political fences mended. Heck was obviously a different kind of cat.

"I'm grateful for that, Chief."

"Tread carefully, but don't be afraid of blowback. Follow procedure, and go wherever the leads take you."

"I will."

As she rose to leave, Heck said, "And take care of yourself, Murphy."

She nodded mutely and left the office wondering if there were rumors that she was drinking too much.

Watson was waiting in her office. "Well, what was that all about?"

She told him about her conversation with the Chief.

"Damn," he said. "Paul Dillon called to complain that we're investigating his son's murder?"

"Crazy, isn't it? In all the time since we first spoke with him he never contacted us once to ask if we were making progress. But when we get a lead and ask for his help, he complains to the Chief."

"Don't that beat all?"

"I'm beginning to really believe there is something in Apelbaum's story that led to murder, and it has something to do with Wakefield and the Russians."

"I think so, too, but we have damn all to go on. Nobody's talking, and we can't make 'em."

Michael R. Davidson

"And don't forget Bob Strachey. He asks a few questions around town and finds some creep following him."

"This is beginning to sound spooky."

"Spooky? Does that mean something in Southern speak?"

"Nope. I mean spooks – spies."

"Shit, I hope not. Espionage and politics. Nothing is ever simple in this damned town where either of those is concerned. Washington is like a dark, slimy cave with side tunnels running off in all directions. No matter where you turn, you risk falling into a deep hole."

Watson shook his head. "Democracy in action. Didn't someone say it's the worst form of government?"

"Churchill. The worst form of government except for all the rest. But they say Washington is a swamp, and in two hundred years it's accumulated a lot of muck."

"And a lot of dangerous critters under the water. Do you think we'll ever get to the bottom of whatever led to Dugan's murder and the others?"

"Not if we don't get a break sometime soon. Maybe Strachey will come up with something."

"Yeah, if somebody doesn't shoot him first."

CHAPTER 15

Robert Strachey resumed trolling for information around town. And he also resumed an old habit of not leaving the house unarmed. In his case the weapon of choice was an ancient Walther PP, a slick, compact German semi-automatic that he carried in a small holster that fit inside his waistband. It was, of course, impossible to carry it on his numerous lobbying visits to Capital Hill and other federal buildings in Washington. Otherwise, he was packing.

The Metropolitan Club is located at 1700 'H' Street in Washington, DC. It's been in the same location since 1863, though the present building was constructed in 1908. The membership is distinguished, and its dining room is renowned for excellent cuisine. While waiting for his guest, three ambassadors, two generals, and a TV personality walked past Strachey into the dining room.

Strachey had invited an old Agency acquaintance, Barton Graham, to lunch with him. Graham was a legendary Cold Warrior with vast experience working against the Soviets. He'd retired in the nineties to teach and write.

As usual, Graham was punctual and approached Strachey with the careful articulation of the elderly. Like Harvey Grant, he appeared frailer than ever, and Strachey computed that he must be in his mid-eighties. None of his wit and intelligence had abandoned him, however.

Strachey waited until they were finishing the main course of lump crabcakes to broach the subject that interested him. "What do you think of George Wakefield, Barton?"

Graham laid down his fork and chewed the last of his crabcake before answering. "What do you mean? Do I like the man? No. Was he a capable intelligence officer? Yes, although he had a penchant for taking unnecessary risks. He and the Agency did not part on amicable terms."

"But he rose pretty high."

"Yes, he had some remarkable accomplishments, but he was too flashy, too controversial. Once he had real power, he abused it. Why are you interested in George Wakefield?"

Barton Graham was one of those people that demanded the sort of respect that made it impossible to lie to him. "I'm doing a favor for a friend," said Strachey, "a police detective friend."

Graham cocked an eyebrow and repeated, "'A police detective friend?' Is George in some kind of legal trouble?"

"No, not yet anyway."

"Then why are the police interested in him?"

"Erm, it's the Dugan Dillan murder investigation. There may be some sort of Russian connection involving Wakefield's firm, but nobody's talking. I think my friend turned to me out of desperation because I'm former Agency like Wakefield, and I agreed to ask around informally. The cop is a good friend."

"It seems a strange way for the police to operate."

"The police don't know the people I know."

"Have you discovered anything?"

"Not much. Everybody has an opinion of George Wakefield, either strongly in favor or strongly against."

"I see."

Graham was not being particularly forthcoming, which was not unusual. Years of experience in an arcane field had taught him to think before he spoke.

The waiter came to clear their plates, and they ordered the club's famous macaroons and coffee for dessert.

"You know," said Graham, "that many of my former colleagues stay in touch with me." What he meant was that the people who used to work under him who now held senior positions often sought his counsel. Thus he remained privy to a lot that was happening at Langley. He belonged to that level of old boys that never really leave the fold because their knowledge always would be valuable. The words hinted that more was to come. Graham wasn't shutting him down.

"Yes," said Strachey. He waited while the older man took a careful sip of coffee.

"You have a good reputation, Bob. I was sad and baffled when you left the Agency. Harvey Grant and many others think the world of you, and I think I can trust your discretion."

But even his old friend, Harvey Grant, had refused to say anything on the subject of a possible Russian connection of George Wakefield. Strachey wondered if Harvey had spoken to Graham since then. He had the sense of stepping into deep water.

Graham continued, "You must be very careful about how you use what I'm about to tell you. And be mindful that I can't tell you everything. First, George Wakefield does have ties to Russia, or at least his firm does. He's been retained for some time to represent one of the so-called *siloviki*, strong men who were once in the KGB. He's been in Moscow a couple of times that we know of, and maybe more. His primary contact there is a banker named Avraham Golubov. Occasionally Wakefield is visited here by a prominent Moscow attorney with known FSB connections. The general opinion is that the Russians hired him to work on getting the economic sanctions we've imposed on Russia and on certain prominent Russian citizens and institutions removed. Russia is not in good financial shape these days with an economy mostly dependent on oil and gas."

"Is there more?"

"Not that I can say, but it should be enough to get you started."

That was it. Graham turned his attention to the large macaroon dessert. That was all Strachey was going to get on the subject of George Wakefield.

Confirmation that Wakefield had Russian contacts was valuable, although nothing Graham had said suggested illegal activity. Still, behind his words hovered the certainty that Langley was interested in whatever was going on, and that was significant.

Strachey had not mentioned that someone had been following him or that he'd sent his family out of town.

He didn't see anyone behind him as he drove back to his 'K' Street office. He'd call Krystal Murphy and set up a meeting after work.

CHAPTER 16

They met in a little bar on Route 7, Krystal, Watson, and Strachey.

"Well, that's news, at least," said Krystal after Strachey's recitation of what Barton Graham had said. "Maybe we should see Wakefield again and this time ask about the Russians."

Strachey was surprised. "You didn't ask the first time?"

"I wanted to gather some more facts before we touched it. Maybe it was a mistake."

Maybe it was, maybe it wasn't. Strachey wasn't sure. "The kind of work Graham described would require legal representation beyond what Wakefield himself could provide. What do you want to bet that Paul Dillon is part of this?"

"More to the point," said Krystal, "I'll bet Dugan Dillan was involved. Put that together with Apelbaum's claims, and we'd be getting somewhere."

"I still don't get it," said Watson. "The press is full of stuff about the Russkies interfering in elections and all sorts of other stuff about one politician or another, the candidates, shit, everybody."

"So?" asked Krystal.

"So, what is there in all that that would be worth killing three people to keep quiet? Don't you think that's what we have to find out?"

Not for the first time Krystal was impressed by Watson's insightfulness. He'd gone straight to the heart of the matter. "I think I agree," she said. "What do you think, Bob?"

"I think that if Frank is right, your investigation has moved into dangerous territory."

Krystal recalled Watson's suspicions. "Bob, do you think we're dealing with espionage here?"

"Probably." His voice was glum.

She made a sour face. "Well, then, we might just be fucked."

Watson shook his head. "Y'all know the difference between a northern fairy tale and a southern fairy tale?"

Krystal and Strachey stared at him blankly.

"Well," continued Watson, satisfied he had their attention, "a northern fairy tale begins 'once upon a time;' a southern fairy tale begins "you ain't gonna believe this shit."

"You think we're chasing a fairy tale?" asked Krystal.

"Hell no. I just don't believe this shit."

This was welcome comic relief, and Krystal suspected Watson had intuited that they needed to break the grim mood they were sinking into.

"Thanks, Frank," she laughed. "We are indeed stepping into some deep doo-doo."

"You know, Krystal," said Strachey, "Harvey Grant suggested you consult with the FBI. You're still in touch with Enoch Whitehall, aren't you? Something like this might be right up his alley."

"Ah, crap, I hate to go that route, and given what happens every time we ask a question, I doubt Enoch would say anything more than the others, especially if there's a big investigation going on. I don't want to go to him ... yet."

"It's your decision to make," said Strachey. "I

suppose you ought to go back to Wakefield then."

The blonde behind the reception desk peered at them suspiciously and again registered annoyance and disapproval of Krystal's work attire. The big black guy with the polished skull was there again and stared at them expressionlessly as if to say he didn't care whether they lived or died.

"We want to speak with Mr. Wakefield," announced Krystal.

"It's police business," added Watson who was doing his best to stare the black behemoth down.

Again, Wakefield must have seen them on the CCTV monitor. His voice sounded from a speaker on the receptionist's desk. "Bring them on in, Samantha, and hold my next appointment until we're finished." He sounded annoyed.

Samantha stood and straightened her tight skirt, the hem of which was located approximately half-way between her knees and hips. They once again followed her down a hallway as Watson concentrated his attention on the blonde's oscillating derriere. Krystal gave him a sharp elbow to the side, and he slid his eyes in her direction and winked.

Wakefield remained seated when they entered and waved them into a couple of chairs in front of his desk. "I thought I made it clear the last time that I know nothing about Dugan Dillon's death. I can't imagine what more you expect from me."

By pre-arrangement Watson spoke first. "Well, Mr. Wakefield, since our first visit we've learned that you've been messin' around with a bunch of Russkies.

Is that right?"

Wakefield's eyes widened slightly before his face closed down. "I have several foreign clients," he said softly as he shifted his gaze from Watson to Krystal.

"Was Dugan Dillon in any way involved with the Russian clients?" asked Krystal holding Wakefield's eyes with a steady gaze.

It was impossible to read Wakefield's face. This was a man who had perfected the art of revealing nothing over decades of experience with the CIA.

"No," said Wakefield, "he was not."

"Could his murder be in any way connected with your work with the Russians?" she persisted, still holding his gaze.

"Absolutely not." Wakefield displayed white teeth in a tight smile that was not quite a smile. "If that's all you came to ask, there's nothing more, and I have a busy day ahead." He stood to dismiss them.

Krystal wasn't finished. "Are you working on Russia's behalf to get sanctions lifted?"

Wakefield's smile disappeared. "There is nothing wrong with representing our clients' interests. I'm even registered as an agent, all nice and legal. Why don't you check it?"

"Your firm does opposition research for politicians, doesn't it?"

"Everybody knows that, too. Now you're boring me." Wakefield remained standing.

They weren't going to get anything more from him. She stood and Watson followed suit. "We can find our way out. Thank you for now. We'll contact you again if it becomes necessary."

The heat and humidity of the late morning hit

them like a wall when they emerged onto the street. They inhaled the scent of Washington in summer, hot rubber, hot exhaust fumes, hot concrete, hot air, and hot money. People think the center of power in Washington is the White House or the Capitol, but they're wrong. It's on 'K' Street where the lobbyists roost in glass-fronted eyries and distribute their largesse among the city's many outstretched hands.

They'd parked in a no parking zone near-by, leaving a sign on the dashboard announcing they were on official police business. In the short while they'd been in Wakefield's office, the interior had risen to a Sahara-like temperature, and she cranked the air conditioning to maximum as soon as the engine turned over.

"What do you think?" she asked.

"Did you notice how his face turned red toward the end?"

"Yeah. He was either getting angry or alarmed. Hard to tell."

"I'd say both. We touched a nerve."

CHAPTER 17

As the sun rose, so did Robert Strachey. He donned an old pair of shorts, a CIA t-shirt and running shoes. A few minutes later, he stepped out of his front door to begin his daily three-mile jog. He didn't run fast, but he kept up a fair trot as he navigated the nearly empty streets of his neighborhood.

His route took him southwest, across Chain Bridge Road toward Lewinsville Park where he usually did several laps around the perimeter of the playing fields. He liked to think when he was running. The uptake of oxygen cleared his mind and he could concentrate. His body was on automatic pilot, pumping his legs, swinging his arms, and synchronizing his breathing with his stride.

This morning he was thinking about his meeting with Barton Graham. What was it Graham had said? "... be mindful that I can't tell you everything." So the veteran CIA officer was admitting he knew something more than what he had said, but how much, and why had he said anything at all? The man was the soul of discretion, and yet he had volunteered the information on Wakefield's ties to Russia. Maybe Harvey Grant had spoken to him. Maybe he had come to the meeting prepared to pass the information along. Something was going on, something heavy.

Strachey was running along the left margin of Chain Bridge Road on his return route and didn't hear the car approaching from behind until it was nearly too late. Something made him look back over his shoulder and he saw a heavy sedan bearing down on him at high speed. The car had crossed the center line into the oncoming lane and climbed onto the shoulder behind him. Strachey barely had time to dive to the side into the thick shrubbery before the car sped past. It made no attempt to stop but swerved back into the proper lane and disappeared in the distance.

Bruised, scratched by brambles, and breathing hard, Strachey picked himself up. He hadn't carried his Walther for the morning run, but it would have done him no good in any event.

He limped home, watchful for another attempt and half expecting to find someone waiting for him at the house. He approached cautiously but saw nothing. He unlocked the front door and slipped inside, immediately grabbing the Walther from the side table just inside the entrance. Fifteen minutes later he sat on the side of his bed having checked the house thoroughly.

Well, he said to himself, *it seems I've touched a nerve.*

After a quick, hot shower he pulled on a pair of khakis and an old blue dress shirt. He would miss work today. After informing his office that he would not be in, he checked his car for booby traps before backing into the street and heading for Arlington.

Krystal wasn't in when Strachey arrived at Police Headquarters, but he found Watson lounging in a chair nursing a cup of coffee.

"This's the first time I've seen you wear anything

Michael R. Davidson

but a suit," said the Georgia native. "I was beginning to think you didn't have any regular clothes." Then he noticed the bruise on Strachey's temple and the scratches on his arms. "What happened to you?"

Strachey pointed to Watson's coffee. "You have any more of that?"

"Sure you want coffee? You look a little wound up."

"I'm sure."

"Okie dokie. Ya'll just make yourself comfy and I'll fetch you a cup of the Arlington PD's finest."

Strachey eyed him suspiciously. "Are you being a wise-ass?"

Watson took no offense. "Nope, just hospitable like my mama taught me." He went out into the common area and returned with steaming black coffee in a heavy, navy mug. "Wanna tell me what's going on with you?"

When Strachey finished recounting the morning's events Watson lost his normally relaxed air. "Shit," he said. "That's a helluva way to start the day."

"No kidding. I wasn't able to get the license or see the driver. It could have been the same car I saw at my house the other day, but who knows?"

"Hell's bells," said Watson. "This Dillon case is getting hotter than a hooker's doorknob on nickel night."

Strachey had to smile at that fine turn of phrase. "I haven't heard anybody say that since I was a kid."

"Well, it seemed appropriate."

"I agree. Something big is going on here, bigger than we can imagine, bigger than us maybe. Where's

Krystal? She needs to hear this because all three of us had better be very, very careful from here on out."

"She got called over to see Chief Heck again. Should be back soon."

A half hour later, Krystal burst into the office looking worried and angry.

"What's wrong, Red?" asked Watson rising from his chair.

"You won't believe what's going on," she replied.

"Neither will you," said Strachey, who was in a chair beside the door. She hadn't noticed him when she came in.

She turned toward him. "What are you doing here?"

"You first."

What she really needed at that moment was a drink. She was actually trembling in anger. Again, she wished she were a smoker.

"Chief Heck has been getting more calls   ... including from two Senators and the Congressman from this District. It seems that Paul Dillon's been whining to them that we're harassing him and his clients."

Watson grimaced. "So Heck told you to lay off?"

She flopped into the chair behind the desk and laid her hands on it to stop the trembling. "No. He said to go full steam ahead. He told the politicos he has an investigation to run, and he intends to do it. Apparently, they weren't happy with his answer and threatened to go over his head."

"To the County Board?"   Watson was incredulous.

"Who the fuck knows," she said, "Maybe the

Michael R. Davidson

White House will call next. But our new Chief has
some backbone. He's not been here long enough to be
infected by the politics."

Watson shook his head. "In that case, he
probably won't last long."

"Then we'd better wrap this thing up before
someone drops the hammer on him."

Strachey interjected, "There have been other
new developments."

She'd almost forgotten about him. "Such as?"

"Someone tried to kill me today and damned
near succeeded. We've struck a nerve somewhere."

She gaped in astonishment, and his injuries
registered with her for the first time. "Tried to kill
you? How?"

When he finished talking the room fell silent.
Watson and Strachey waited for her to speak.

"Well," she said after a couple of beats, "at least
they didn't try to shoot you like the others."

"I've been thinking about that," said Strachey.
"Assuming it was the same people, they decided to
switch their M.O. Another shooting connected to the
Dillon case would have looked suspicious to everyone
and raised more questions. A hit and run would look
random."

"That's logical," she said. "But I don't like it
that you've been targeted."

"I'll be fine," he said, "but I suggest you two
start looking over your shoulders."

Krystal had been the target of two attempted
murders in the past and barely escaped with her life.
She turned a concerned face to Watson. "Frank, I'm
worried about your family."

"I'll have Emily take the kids out of school for a few days and keep her eyes peeled. I'm not worried about her. Emily's a country girl. She knows her way around guns, and we have a bunch of' 'em at home. They'll be OK, providing we can put an end to all this soon."

Krystal thought Watson was taking it too casually. "You'd better go home now and talk to Emily. I don't want to take any more chances."

It was bad enough that Strachey had been targeted, and she again felt a pang of guilt for involving him, at all.

"If you say so, Red."

After Watson left, Krystal invited Strachey to lunch. She felt a compelling need to get out of the office to someplace quiet.

Thirty minutes later they settled into a booth at an Irish watering hole far out on Wilson Boulevard. Krystal broke her long-standing rule and ordered a double scotch along with her beer. She hoped the alcohol would settle her nerves. Things were spinning out of control, and she didn't see that they could do any more than they already were doing. The trouble was they were running into dead-ends and people kept getting killed, or having someone try to kill them. They needed something to break their way.

Strachey watched her down the scotch in a single swallow. "Whoa," he said, "Better take it easy there." It had been Strachey who introduced her to scotch. He was a confirmed single malt man, but he didn't drink before six P.M.

"It'll settle my nerves." She was both defensive and embarrassed. She didn't like her friends to see her like this. Not even Ray Velazquez knew she had graduated to solitary drinking. At least she hoped no one had noticed. Worse, she worried that the drinking might be slowing her down, making her dull.

She knew there must be a deep-seated reason, but it remained elusive. Maybe it was boredom. Maybe it was fear. Whatever it was, she was ashamed because it made her feel weak.

CHAPTER 18

It was still early afternoon when Krystal returned to the office with Strachey. Watson was still out.

She'd drawn no inspiration from their conversation over lunch. She had been too distracted by her momentary weakness to concentrate. She'd slipped up and now felt foolish, something guaranteed not to improve her mood which was fading from blue to black. Had Strachey detected the crack in her veneer? She'd never thought of herself as putting up a front, hiding behind a façade. She had no use for façades. What you saw was what you got with Krystal Murphy. But now she had a guilty secret to hide, and it was no one's fault but her own.

Strachey chose a chair in front of her desk and sat there fidgeting. He wanted something to happen, something to break in the case, all the more so because someone had very nearly taken his life and might well try again. In fact, he was angry.

Krystal pretended to look through the papers on her desk, not really seeing them and was startled by a knock at the door. A uniform was standing there with a large envelope in his hand. "This just arrived for you from AT&T."

It took her a moment to remember they'd issued a warrant for Alex Apelbaum's phone records.

"Thanks," she said and ripped open the manila envelope. Inside was a compilation of all the calls on Alex Apelbaum's phone for a period of two weeks leading up to his murder.

Michael R. Davidson

Strachey straightened up in his chair. "Let's split them up. We'll get through it faster."

"I'm going to concentrate on the calls beginning a few days before he published the article," she said. "I don't think he sat on the story longer than that."

She went down the list, drawing her finger down the left-hand margin to keep her place. It didn't take ten minutes for her to find what she was looking for, and she couldn't keep the excitement from her voice.

"Look at this. It can't be a coincidence."

Strachey looked at the entry to which she was pointing. "What is it?" he asked.

"Look at the address," breathed Krystal. "Walden Drive – the Dillons' house is on that street."

"It's a cell phone," said Strachey.

"I don't recognize the name, but it must be one of the neighbors."

"You need to talk to them. This may be the break we've been waiting for."

"Damn right. Too bad we don't have a transcipt of the conversation."

"You'll have to be satisfied with the meta data."

She gave him a questioning look. "Meta data? Like in the news?"

"Yes. That's what you have there in the call records. Every phone company stores meta data. Oh, the associated conversation is probably out there someplace, most likely at NSA. But you'll never get your hands on it."

"I have a powerful friend at the FBI." She was thinking of Enoch Whitehall.

"It doesn't matter. They would never release it to you. It's out of bounds."

"Whitehall has done favors for me before."

"You are aware, aren't you, of the shitstorm in Washington over NSA's programs and the way politicians and the press have been using them? Your friend Whitehall isn't about to dip his hands into that cesspool, not even for you."

"Then we need to talk to this neighbor pronto."

Strachey nodded. "You know, there has to be some very strong reasons Paul Dillon is holding back information. Dugan was his son, after all. The incentives to keep silent have overridden his fatherly instincts. Those incentives have to be either positive or negative."

"You mean either someone is threatening him or he was in on his own son's murder."

"Something like that. And when you take into consideration the pressure being put on Chief Heck the only conclusion is that whatever it is, it's big, very nasty, and very political. When and if this case breaks into the open there'll be hell to pay for someone."

There was no denying the logic of Strachey's reasoning. She'd experienced political pressure before, but nothing on this scale.

"You're probably right," she said. "But all we can do is follow the leads."

"Let's hope we don't follow them to our graves," he said.

CHAPTER 19

Krystal left the car at the curb and walked to the front door of the house directly across the street from the Dillon residence. Watson had not returned to the office, and Krystal didn't want to wait another day before interviewing the owner of the cell phone.

A petite young woman of Katherine Dillon's age answered her ring. The records identified the owner of the cell phone as Melodie Crane, and they confirmed that this was she.

"Mrs. Crane," said Krystal, "may I come in for a chat?"

It was a neat house filled with expensive, modern furniture, and they took seats in front of a large, natural stone fireplace in the living room.

Melodie Crane was an attractive brunette with startlingly blue eyes and a milky complexion that matched her British accent. She wore neat, white slacks and a red blouse. A diamond tennis bracelet adorned her wrist. Interestingly, she had not expressed surprise at a visit from the police. She sat quietly with her hands in her lap waiting for Krystal to speak.

"Mrs. Crane, I'm here in connection with the investigation into Dugan Dillon's murder."

"Of course," said Melodie, "I thought so. I'll help in any way I can."

"Do you know the Dillons well?"

"Yes, Katherine is my best friend. We both moved into the neighborhood at the same time, and we've been close ever since, and our kids always played together."

"Mrs. Crane, do you know a man named Alex Apelbaum?"

Melodie crinkled her forehead and shook her head. "No. I don't think so."

Krystal speared her with a hard look. "Then why did you call him on your cell phone."

Melodie crossed her arms and said, "I didn't."

"Cell phone records say differently."

"Wait a minute," said Melodie, "My cell phone? But I don't have it anymore. I lent it to Katherine, and she never gave it back."

"When did this happen?"

"Oh, I don't know. Several days ago? I thought it was odd. I visited her last week, but she acted strangely. I suppose she must still be suffering terribly. She just wasn't herself and that horrible woman shooed me right out of the house."

"What horrible woman."

"I don't know her name. She looked Latino, and she just stood behind Katherine glaring at me all the time."

"You mean the nanny?"

"Nanny? Katherine never had a nanny. I'd never seen that woman before. I tried to see Katherine several times over the past month or so, but could hardly get past the door. The last time, Katherine answered. She stepped outside and closed the door before that woman could reach us and asked if she could borrow my cell phone. I gave it to her, and she put it in her pocket just before that woman opened the door. It was very strange."

"She never had a nanny?"

"No. Katherine is very involved with raising her children. She's not the sort of person who would want anyone between them and her. But we haven't seen the children since Dugan's death. They were taken out of school right after and never came back. Frankly, I've been worried about them and Katherine."

"You didn't say anything when police interviewed you right after the murder." Krystal had had the uniforms canvass the neighborhood after the initial interview with Katherine Dillon, but no leads had come of it.

"Well, that was before I'd even had a chance to offer condolences. The whole street was in shock. The Dillons were well-liked."

"When did you last see Katherine?"

"When I gave her my phone. I was going to go over today to ask for it back."

Krystal rose. "Thank you, Mrs. Crane. You've been a great help." She couldn't leave fast enough.

Driven by newly born urgency, she rushed across the street to the Dillon house. This time there were no cars in the drive, and the garage doors were closed. There was no response to her repeated pounding on the front door. She slipped between the shrubbery and the wall to get a glimpse through a window. Inside, all was dark. Nothing moved.

She walked around the house and still could detect no signs of life, which made her nervous. The rear of the house was dominated by a large, wooden deck that looked out over a fenced yard with a swing set and a couple of old growth trees and a lot of flowering plants. The lawn looked unattended, as had the front, with grass several inches beyond what must be a height acceptable to the homeowners association.

Access to the deck was via French doors. She made a decision. It would be much better, and safer, if she had waited for Watson to accompany her, but she had to get into the house. If what Melodie Crane said was true, Katherine Dugan and her children could be in mortal danger ... or worse.

She tried the French doors, but they were deadbolted, so the only recourse was to break a pane and reach inside to unlock them. A small bin beside the doors contained gardening tools, and she selected a trowel with a solid metal handle to break the glass.

Beretta held before her, she entered the darkened house, fearful of what she might find. She could imagine finding three bodies, one large, two small, lying in pools of congealed blood. But there was nothing. She searched both floors and the basement. The garage was empty. She discovered only signs of hurried packing in the master bedroom where the closets and drawers had been left open.

As if three dead men and the attempted murder of Strachey were not enough, she was certain the case had entered another dimension – the disappearance of a woman and her two children. While it was possible that Katherine Dillon had left on her own, the ersatz nanny more likely was the cause. Mercedes Unduragga, if that was her real name, had assumed a menacing character. Krystal could at least be grateful there were no more bodies ... yet.

She called Watson on his cell, filled him in, and instructed him to get the forensics unit to the Dillon house as soon as possible.

CHAPTER 20

"Don't you think you're getting a little ahead of yourself, Red?"

Fully charged with adrenalin, Krystal didn't at first understand Watson's question.

"Just calm down a little," he continued. "I heard what you said, and you may well be right, but it's also possible that Katherine left on her own. Or maybe she's visiting her folks or the Dillons."

Of course, he was right. She'd jumped to conclusions not yet supported by facts. The only new information she had was that Mercedes Undurraga was not the family's nanny, at least not before Dugan's death.

It was embarrassing. They'd been chasing their tails and anything new glimmered like fools gold. This was rookie behavior. The adrenalin deserted her like rats from a sinking ship. She could almost feel it flowing out through her toes.

Abashed, she said, "You're right, Frank."

"So you broke into the house?"

"Yeah, I did. I broke a window."

"Well, I think you were justified. I would'a done the same thing."

"Really?"

"Yeah. After what you learned about that woman. Anything might have happened."

She felt a little better and resolved not to let go of her suspicions without doing some checking first. "Listen, Frank, I still want a squad car posted out here in front of the house. Coordinate with the Fairfax

County guys. They can handle it, or we'll do it. Bottom line - nobody gets in except Katherine Dillon."

"No problem, Red. You going back to the office?"

"I guess. I want to make some calls to see if Paul Dillon or anybody else knows where Katherine and the kids are."

"I'll meet you there."

"No need. I'll see you there in the morning. I'm going to ask around the neighborhood if anyone saw them leave. Can you try to get in touch with Paul Dillon?"

"Sure."

She spent the next hour going from house to house and was rewarded by an elderly man who said he never went to bed before two in the morning. He'd seen the Dillon SUV leaving the neighborhood around one A.M. He hadn't noticed who was in the car.

It was a strange time for Katherine to have taken her children for a drive.

Katherine Dillon's parents lived in Arizona according to Melodie Crane, who supplied them with their phone number. They had no idea where their daughter and grandchildren might be, and it was clear they were apprehensive despite being told it was "only a routine check." A call from the police about a loved one is never routine.

It was early afternoon by the time they pulled to a stop at Paul Dillon's residence. Finding the attorney and arranging a meeting had not been easy. His office said he wasn't there and was not forthcoming about when he might be in. It had taken some aggressive questioning bordering on threats to get the lawyer's home phone number and address.

Krystal decided not to call Dillon himself beforehand, even though his office would likely warn the lawyer.

The residence turned out to be a palatial pile of red bricks and white stucco along Route 7 west towards Winchester, Virginia. It was fronted by acres of fenced pasture land that contained several horses. There was a barn and separate stables, as well as a small log house that might have served for workers or been the original building on the land. The restoration of old log houses was a growing trend.

The house was approached via a long, gravelled private road leading to a circular macadamed drive with a fountain in the middle. The front portico was supported by four round pillars of impressive girth, and a massive set of steps led up to the terraced entrance which Watson said was "a helluva front porch."

They parked the Challenger and climbed the steps to a set of double doors. There was a doorbell, so Watson stabbed it with his finger, and they waited.

They waited a long time, but after five minutes and repeated rings and knocks, the door was finally opened by Paul Dillon himself. Krystal had half expected to be confronted by a uniformed butler or maid.

Dillon was bleary-eyed and slightly disheveled, like a man who had not slept for a long time. He was dressed in suit pants and a wrinkled white shirt open at the neck, and his silver hair was no longer carefully coiffed. This was not the powerful, self-assured man Krystal had first encountered with Chief Fogerty two months ago.

Dillon regarded them with suspicious eyes. "What do you want?" His voice was rough, edged with fatigue.

"Is your daughter-in-law here with you?" asked Krystal.

"No, she's not."

Still the lawyer's response – answer the question and say no more. But there was no hostility in his voice this time. If anything, there was fatigue and maybe a hint of fear. And he did not seem curious about the reason they were asking.

"Do you know where she and the children are?"

Dillon hesitated before replying. "They're away. She decided she needed a break."

"Where did they go?"

Some of the old defiance returned. "That doesn't concern you."

She didn't back down. "Sir, we have reason to believe Katherine may be in trouble. We need to know she's safe. Please tell us how to contact her."

Dillon's voice regained some strength. "Katherine is entitled to her privacy, and I don't want her disturbed by more questions. I'll not have you hounding the poor girl any more. Now, leave my property."

He started to close the door, but Krystal stopped him. "Why won't you cooperate, Mr. Dillon? Your son was murdered yet you've done nothing to help us find his killer. What are you afraid of?"

"Go away," he said. "Just go away and leave us

in peace." He closed the door.

"Do you think they're here?" asked Watson as they descended the steps to the car. "It's a big place."

"If they were here, it would have been easier to let us see them, no matter how much they might resent it. Dillon's too smart not to know how suspicious his refusal to cooperate makes him look. No, something else is going on, and whatever it is, Dillon is scared."

"Yeah. I thought so too. Looked like he'd been rode hard an put away wet. Something's going on, alright."

"It's looking more and more probable that Katherine and the kids have been kidnapped or taken hostage. I've seen that kind of behavior before in kidnapping cases."

"What are you going to do, Red?"

"First thing is get a forensics unit into that house. I think we have enough to get a warrant. And we'd better act fast before Dillon can call on his buddies to stymie us."

Back on Route 7 she turned on the strobes and mashed the accelerator. She'd need Chief Heck's support on this, for sure. One hand on the wheel, she punched the speed dial for Heck's office and filled him in.

"Jesus, Krystal," said the Chief. "What the hell are we getting into here?"

She liked his use of the word "we" and hoped he wouldn't go wobbly on them now. "Can you help us get a warrant, Chief?"

"What the hell? You've got grounds, and I'll try to find a friendly judge."

CHAPTER 21

They were gathered at Strachey's place where they sat around the kitchen table. Strachey had prepared sandwiches and set out tubs of delicatessen potato salad and coleslaw. It was well after six o'clock, so there was also a bottle of Lagavulin and three glasses, along with chilled green bottles of Grolsch beer.

Forensics had sent the fingerprints lifted from the Dillon house to the FBI's Criminal Justice Services Division, the national repository of fingerprints and other biometric data. It could be several days before a response would be received.

Strachey poured the Lagavulin and said, "Let's review what you have so far. It always helps to re-consider the outlines of the big picture, at least the parts we know about. First, Dugan Dillon is murdered in the county club parking lot. His widow claims to know nothing, and his father offers no help. Weeks pass before that article appears on the web, based on an anonymous tip. You question Alex Apelbaum, and the same night, he and his friend are shot down at their apartment complex. Forensics tells us the same gun that killed Dugan was used this time, as well. But the article suggests that Dugan was involved with the Wakefield Group in lobbying for the Russians. Wakefield says he knows nothing, but you do get the small admission that Dugan did some work for the firm. Paul Dillon finally admits the same, but both claim the work was unimportant. The motive for Dugan's murder is still unclear. I start digging around town for info on what Wakefield might be up to with the Russians. Next thing, I find myself being followed and then damn near get run over. You learn that it must have been Katherine Dillon who gave the tip about the Russians to Apelbaum, but she's disappeared, maybe taken against her will, along with the erzatz nanny."

"Yep," said Watson. "That's about it. It's surely the deepest shit I've ever waded through."

"Mysteries within mysteries," mused Strachey. "I'd say there's a lot more than murder going on here. I really don't like the Russian angle."

"You mean you don't think the Russian connection is really so important?" Krystal asked.

Strachey shook his head and drained his Lagavulin. He poured himself another. "Quite the opposite; this sounds like something the Russians could very well be mixed up in. Unsolved murders is a Russian speciality. The news is full of allegations of Russian 'active measures' in Washington. It wouldn't be the first time they've resorted to wet work to cover their tracks."

Watson squinted at him. "Wet work?"

"Murder," said Strachey. "The Russians resort to it frequently to silence troublesome people."

Watson sipped the Lagavulin and made a face. "You got any bourbon, Bob?"

"Sure, Makers Mark do?"

Watson smiled a big smile. "Now you're talkin'. But you know, about this Russian business – it's pretty hairy stuff. I'm not sure we're up to it. We might need some help."

He looked from Strachey to Krystal. "What do

you think, Red?"

She'd been sipping the Lagavulin, resisting the urge to down the entire glass. She was still embarrassed by her earlier slip with Strachey, and she wasn't going to repeat the mistake. But it wasn't easy.

"You think we should get the feebies involved? Is that what you're trying to say?"

Strachey replied, "That's up to you, kid. What I do know, or have good reason to suspect, is that the CIA has picked up some vibes but can't or won't come clean. I think Barton Graham was instructed to steer us onto the right path, but there was a limit to what he could say."

He rummaged in a cabinet for the bourbon while Krystal chewed over his words. She was personally invested in this case now. They were finally onto something, and she wanted to solve it herself. She'd not hesitated to seek the FBI's help, or at least the help of Enoch Whitehall, in the past and wondered if she was being too tight-assed now. The FBI could well take the entire case right out of her hands, and she wanted to be in at the grand finale, dammit. She finished her Lagavulin, relishing its deep, smoky essence, and held out her glass for another. The hell with appearances.

Chief Heck received a barrage of blistering phone calls protesting the forensics examination of Katherine Dillon's house. The Chief was beginning to wither under the abuse.

"Hang on, Chief," she'd told him. "Things will break soon."

"Let's hope so. This is getting ridiculous."

What might be a break came in the form of a letter requesting Krystal's presence at a meeting with Executive Assistant Director for Counter Intelligence Enoch Whitehall. The only reason she could think of was to discuss the findings of the Criminal Justice Services Division. The invitation pre-emped her decision on whether to approach Whitehall. But that wasn't the biggest surprise.

She'd only seen the enigmatic FBI legend a few times anywhere outside his office. Communications with him had usually been by telephone. But here was a letter, written in a spidery hand from the man himself inviting her to meet him at an address in the Kalorama section of Northwest Washington. The missive had been posted the day before, and the meeting was set for this evening.

And there was another surprise.

Robert Strachey quit his job on 'K' Street.

"Well," he announced somewhat sheepishly, "I didn't like the job anyway."

He'd reluctantly accepted the job from his uncle who ran the 'K' Street lobbying firm after resigning from the CIA. He had a growing family to support, and his uncle had regularly importuned him over the years to join him. He didn't like the work, but he was good at it. CIA officers are trained to sway opinions, convince people to do things, such as commit treason, that they otherwise would never do. Lobbying politicians in Congress was a walk in the park by comparison.

But his uncle had received communications from some very influencial people who warned him that his nephew had blotted his copybook. The only explanation was his inquiries about Wakefield. His uncle had offered to resist the pressure, but for Strachey it was a way out of the Washington merry-go-round he hated, maybe less than graceful, but he took it. His uncle had been very generous with his separation package, and he'd made a lot, really a lot, of money. Quitting would not place him in financial straits. He counted himself fortunate.

"You got fired?" Krystal again questioned her judgement in asking for his help. Here was another sacrifice to her selfish ambition.

"Don't fret, kid," said Strachey. "Believe it or not, this is a good thing. And if I'm no longer a Washington pimp, I no longer have to deal with the whores and their Johns." It was perhaps an extreme view of lobbying in Washington, but it was accurate as far as Strachey was concerned.

"I'm really sorry, Bob. I don't know what to say."

"Say I can still help you on this case. You can be Wyatt Earp, and I'll be Doc Holliday."

"Are you sure?"

"Hell, yes. This is the best I've felt in years."

Robert and his wife, Amy, had become close friends via some life-changing events a few years ago. In fact, she had become nearly a member of the family. Amy's father, the indefatigable Thomas Jefferson Dawson, never tired of playfully flirting with her. In return, she'd nearly gotten her friend killed.

CHAPTER 22

The address Enoch Whitehall provided for the meeting was on a quiet street a few blocks north of Massachusetts Avenue. This was prime real estate in the vicinity of Embassy Row, and the homes lining the streets, old Washington mansions, had prices guaranteed to keep the riff-raff at a safe distance. Surveying the place as she left her car, Krystal wondered if this was Whitehall's home. It could well be some sort of FBI safehouse held over from another era. The house was comprised of three stories encased in white stucco with a circular paved drive that passed under a porte-cochere. Twilight was fast giving way to darkness, and light shone from the windows.

She'd abandoned her work clothes for a forest green tailored skirt and jacket and heels, had actually styled her hair to fall softly over her shoulders, and wore a string of pearls, a gift from Ray Velazquez. Somehow, Whitehall's summons demanded a certain formality. She'd left her Beretta at home, but her .380 was snuggled in the small purse she carried.

There was a wrought iron bell pull beside the oak plank front door, and she gave it a tug. Almost immediately the door was opened by a man with a closely cropped fringe of white hair surrounding a shiny pate who could have been sixty or eighty. He wore a black suit and bow tie and exuded the scent of talcum powder and antiquity.

"Miss Murphy," he said and stepped aside to wave her into an entrance hall with an oak-beamed ceiling that towered two stories above their heads. There were niches in the walls containing busts of what looked like Greek philosophers. The floor was a marbled mosaic of the ruins of what she thought must be a Roman amphitheater. Two sets of French doors led off of each side of the hall. She caught a glimpse of a formal dining room on the left – a long polished table with high-backed chairs, sideboards and gilt framed mirrors. Candelabra stood on the table.

The ageless man escorted her to a spacious room on the right which was filled with overstuffed furniture. A large, marble fireplace dominated the room, and oil portraits of American presidents in ornate gold frames hung in an ordered line along wainscoted walls. They walked across a thick, red Persian carpet.

"Please wait here, Miss Murphy. Director Whitehall will join you shortly."

Her gaze wandered around the rich surroundings, and she felt out of place. If this was Whitehall's house, salaries at the FBI must be considerably higher than she'd thought. Maybe he came from old money. There was a surprising number of so-called "dollar a year" men in government service. It was a tradition in certain families. But there were none of the usual Washington rumors about Whitehall's wealth.

These thoughts were interrupted by the entrance of Enoch Whitehall himself, wearing his habitual dark suit. She imagined his wardrobe consisted entirely of black or charcoal gray suits.

The Executive Assistant Director for Counter Intelligence, a man whose name was uttered only in whispers in the halls of Washington, was an old acquaintance. No one could remember when he had not been a fixture at the Bureau. That the only photograph in his office was of him shaking hands with J. Edgar Hoover provided a hint.

The reason for his longevity may lie in the secrets he knew as well as his effectiveness. He'd learned a lot from the first FBI Director, and Hoover's successors gave him a wide birth and considerable independence.

The last time Krystal had visited him, she had been bereft of both gun and badge, and without his help should could well have ended up in the wilderness. She had imagined herself as the single cop in a one-horse town with the primary duty of issuing parking and speeding tickets.

"Good evening, Krystal," said Whitehall in his usual soft, toneless voice.

He looked the same as ever: Gray, not quite white hair, neatly cut and worn in an old-fashioned style, deep-set gray eyes on a hatchet face punctuated by a blade of a nose. The suit hanging on his cadaverous, six foot frame was black over a starched white shirt with a narrow black tie, and highly polished black brogues. He wore no jewelry, not even a wedding band. Krystal again wondered how many such outfits the man possessed as she had never seen him dressed differently.

"Director Whitehall." She stood and extended her hand which he took in his. His hand was warm and dry and his grasp was firm.

He indicated she should sit back down, and he took a chair facing her and crossed his legs. "Thank you for coming on such short notice," he said. "I apologize for the somewhat unorthodox invitation."

"Is this your house, Director?"

A sound that might have been intended as a laugh rattled from his throat. "Oh, no, Krystal. But it is where I live. I have rooms upstairs, as do a half dozen or so other gentlemen of similar circumstances. It's sort of a private residential club for men like me who abhor a more public life."

Krystal looked over his shoulder, half expecting several Whitehall clones to march into the room and stand in a row of alternating black and gray suits, like some sort of otherworldly bar-code. What exactly did he mean by "similar circumstances."

"Don't worry, Krystal, no one will bother us. Our privacy is assured. That's the reason I invited you here rather than to the office – to keep our meeting out of the public eye. In fact, you're the first woman to enter this house in over a dozen years."

The biggest black cat she'd ever seen wandered into the room from the entrance hall and stood stock still when he saw Krystal. Then he padded across the Persian carpet and hopped onto the arm of her chair where he sat and regarded her with yellow eyes. For a fleeting second she thought it might be Whitehall's familiar.

"That's Felix," he said. "He's in charge of rodent control in the house."

The cat turned its attention to Whitehall and meowed in recognition of the introduction. With a final glance at Krystal he leapt from the chair and resumed his patrol back out through the entrance hall.

She hadn't figured the FBI man for an animal lover. "Nice cat," she said.

"Yes. It's very nice of him to permit us to live in his house," he said deadpan.

Krystal assumed this was a joke and smiled.

Whitehall frowned. "Are you alright, Krytsal? If I may say so, I believe you've lost some weight, and you look tired."

She'd avoided the usual drink when she'd gone home to change. But the fact of the matter was that, drink or not, she was tired. She was beginning to feel like that old Al Capp cartoon character, Joe Btfsplk, who was accompanied by a dark rain cloud everywhere he went. Joe was a well-meaning sort, but he brought misfortune to everyone he met.

"I'm OK," she said. "I've just been working a lot."

"May I have Simpson bring you a cup of hot tea? It's quite bracing." His gray eyes, as unreadable as the cat's, didn't leave her, and it was disconcerting.

"No, thanks. I'm fine, really." She lied. She wanted to get down to business before the conversation veered into territory she didn't want the perceptive Whitehall to enter. "Why did you want to see me? I assume it's something official."

He sat back in his chair and steepled his long fingers. "Yes and no," he said. "The request you sent to the Criminal Justice Services Division caused quite a stir at the Bureau and was brought immediately to my attention."

"But that fingerprint request was connected to a criminal case. You're head of counter intelligence – catching spies."

Whitehall'ls lips stretched slightly in his version

of a smile. "Correct, but I'm afraid your case has strayed into my realm, perhaps in more than one way."

Krystal's stomach suddenly felt hollow. This was what she had feared – the case was about to be snatched away by the FBI. "How so?"

Whitehall's expression remained inscrutable. "We'll get to that in good time. First, tell me about this case you're working on and which obviously has you highly frustrated."

This was maddening. The FBI man had called her to the meeting, clearly with some purpose in mind that was, as she had suspected, tied to the request she'd sent to the Bureau to check the fingerprints lifted from Dugan Dillon's house. But she was expected to enlighten him rather than the other way around. She was the fly to Whitehall's spider.

Reading her mind, Whitehall reassured her. "I don't mean to put you at a disadvantage. But I need to know what you know in order to decide the way to go forward. I promise you will leave here tonight with something more than my good will. But, of course, you have that, as well."

"As usual, Director, you're playing a full house to my straight. But I'll oblige you." The man had never lied to her, never let her down. Why should he start now? She filled him in on the investigation to date. He listened with his steepled fingers against his forehead and his eyes closed.

When she had finished he asked, "And you believe Katherine Dillon has been abducted, that she's not voluntarily making herself hard to find?"

"I think so, but the family isn't making any claims to that effect."

Michael R. Davidson

"And you're certain it was Katherine who gave the information to Mr. Apelbaum?"

"She had the cell phone that made the call. I'm sure she knows more than she's told us." She couldn't stop herself asking, "So if it's a kidnapping the FBI will be taking over the case?"

A shadow passed over his eyes, and he looked sad for a fleeting moment. "That would be normal procedure, and something the police would want. But I fear there is nothing normal about this entire matter, and the family has not reported her missing. Tell me, is Robert Strachey still involved?"

"Yes, he refuses to let it drop, especially after someone tried to run him down."

"My old friend Harvey Grant told me he'd tried to dissuade the young man, but feared he had failed. But I somewhat diagree. Strachey may prove to be of considerable value to you, given his special skills. Does he know everything you know?"

She nodded. Krystal did not consider Strachey, who was ten years older than her, to be a "young man," but everything is relative.

"Have you or Officer Watson here been followed, as well?"

"Not that we've noticed. And we're being pretty careful. Strachey too. He sent his family out of town as soon as he spotted surveillance. He thinks whatever is going on is big, big enough to justify murder."

"Robert is a very intelligent and resourceful man."

"So the Bureau really won't take over the case?" She was intrigued that a senior CIA official had been talking to a senior FBI official about Robert Strachey's involvement. It didn't make her feel all warm and safe.

"In a word, no," he answered. "The FBI will not be involved, at least not officially. The fact that you are here tonight talking to me in a completely unofficial, and I might add unauthorized, setting should tell you something."

It was telling her something, alright, something pretty scary. Within a minute it would get a lot more frightening.

Whitehall reached inside his jacket and withdrew a folded sheet of paper. He handed it to her and said, "You are not authorized to see what's in this document. After you've digested it, you will give it back to me."

Half believing her hair would catch fire if she touched it, she took the folded sheet of paper and opened it. The first thing she noticed was the word SECRET stamped in red at the top and bottom. It was in the form of a standard, dryly worded FBI memorandum with a subject line that read "Marisol Klyasnikova." She was described concisely as a Russian attorney involved in lobbying efforts to lift American sanctions against Russia. She was also described as an agent of the FSB. A photocopy of a photograph was superimposed in the middle of the page.

Krystal went cold. The photo was of a younger, but easily identifiable Mercedes Undurraga, the Dillons' nanny.

"Do you understand now why the matter was referred to me?"

She tried to coax some saliva into her mouth.

Michael R. Davidson

"The woman in this picture was introduced to us as a nanny for the children of a murder victim, Dugan Dillon. Now she's disappeared along with Dillon's wife and children."

"This is a serious matter." Whitehall's normally soft voice acquired some resonance. "The Russians have many agents in the United States, but this woman is considerably more than that. We suspect she might even be a staff intelligence officer. Her unusual name is due to the fact that her father was a KGB colonel assigned to Havana where he met and married her Cuban mother some fifty years ago. She's shown up on our radar a few times in the past, in Cuba where she liaised with the DGI, and in Europe. She's also shown up here in the States in the role of legal representative of certain Russian interests. She's a very dangerous individual."

He paused for a beat before concluding, "If she is involved in the disappearance of a woman and two children, I fear they are in grave danger."

"We run into the possibility of some sort of Russian connection to Dugan Dillon's murder every time we turn around. So ..." She trailed into silence.

"Today's Russia is run by former KGB officers," said Whitehall. "They've fallen back into their old habits ... very nasty habits."

"So what happens now?" asked Krystal.

"You continue your investigation," said Whitehall.

"And the FBI won't take over?" He'd already answered this, but she wanted to hear it again.

If it were possible, Whitehall might have looked embarrassed. "Not right now," he said. "There are many people in this town, powerful people, who simply do not want your case to be solved. They want the investigation to go away and be forgotten in a few months. The last thing they want is for the Bureau to get involved. I fear that a dark stain is spreading over Washington."

Mystified, Krystal decided to push further. "Can you tell us anything about George Wakefield? He's involved in some way, but we've come up with nothing solid. He's connected to both the Russians and Dugan Dillon. Dillon's law firm represents Wakefield's outfit. The only thing we're sure about is that we have three murders and one attempted murder, all linked to this case."

Whitehall puffed his cheeks and expelled some air, but he didn't answer her question. "What is your immediate priority?"

Krystal's response was immediate. "To find Katherine Dillon and her children. You said they may be in grave danger."

"Correct. Eventually, I may be able to lend a hand, but not now. In the meantime here is a safe telephone number where I can be reached at any time."

He gave her a folded sheet of note paper with a phone number scrawled in his own hand.

As she was leaving he said, "Don't use that number unless it's absolutely necessary."

She wondered if this was a get out of jail free card. It was very possible she would need one.

CHAPTER 23

The meeting with Enoch Whitehall lasted only an hour, so it wasn't too late to drive out to McLean for a chat with Robert Strachey. She respected the former spook's opinion, and anyway she needed to talk to someone. She was too keyed up to go back to her lonely apartment and hit the sack. She also wanted to avoid the temptation of the bottle waiting in the kitchen cabinet.

She called ahead. After his narrow escape from a hit and run Strachey could have the house rigged with tripwires and claymore mines for all she knew.

The house was in a modest neighborhood by McLean standards, but all the houses there had McLean prices that were not modest. When the baby was born and Amy's father came to live with them, Strachey had thought to buy another place, but his Scots-Irish roots balked at what a bigger house would cost. Instead, he contracted for an addition which consisted of an in-law suite and a nursery.

She made it to the front door without setting off any booby traps. Strachey was waiting for her. "You're looking great tonight, Krystal."

"Thanks, Bob, you're the first person not to ask if I'm feeling ill since I don't know when. Do you mind if I kick off these shoes?"

"Be my guest."

He pointed her to the living room where she dropped the heels onto the floor and bent over to rub her feet. "I hate wearing these things."

"Maybe, but you might try it more often. You

make quite an impression."

"Yeah, sure I do. Listen, we gotta talk."

"I'm glad you came over. I don't think I could have waited 'til morning to hear about your meeting with Whitehall. Would you like a drink?"

Tempting, but she said, "Just an ice water, please."

When he brought the water to her in the living room she saw he had poured himself a whisky, a generous one. She could smell the peat smoke in the Lagavulin and for a second thought about asking him to pour one for her, after all, but she resisted the temptation.

"It was weird. He acted like we were on a top secret mission behind enemy lines. Apparently there are forces at work in Washington to stymie our investigation and everybody wishes it would just go away. Even weirder, I got the impression that these forces are powerful enough to order even the FBI to stand down, and to be fair, this has actually become something the Bureau should be working on."

Strachey whistled softly through his teeth. "I had a feeling we were getting in pretty deep. Does Whitehall want us to back off the case?"

She frowned as she recalled the conversation with the FBI man. "No, quite the opposite. I think he very much wants us to proceed."

"Enoch Whitehall has gone rogue?" Strachey shook his head. "I don't believe it."

"Whatever, he dropped a bombshell – Katherine Dillon's 'nanny' is really a Russian spy. Her real name is Marisol Klyasnikova." It required effort for her to wrap her tongue around the name. "That's what flagged our fingerprint request to Whitehall. He warned me that when the official results are delivered to us, this tidbit won't be included."

Strachey nearly choked on his scotch. "Did he say she's an agent or an officer?"

"What's the difference?"

"There's a big difference between a staff officer and a civilian recruited as an agent. Most people don't understand that."

"He said she could be more than an agent."

"And she's in the States illegally."

"He didn't say that. She's also a lawyer for people who want the sanctions lifted. He said she's been in the country often."

Strachey gulped his scotch and put his glass down. "Didn't we find out that Wakefield has been working to get the sanctions lifted, too? If this woman is a lawyer with the same brief, dollars to donuts she and Wakefield are thick as thieves, and Paul Dillon, too."

"You're right. It's a common thread."

"One thing seems certain: we're working against an intelligence operation, a hostile influence operation. There've been hints of it up until now, but Russian Intel doesn't get involved in petty matters, and they're tough. And I really don't like what Whitehall said about the powers that be in Washington. To me, that means there's a lot of dirt on a lot of people that they would prefer remains secret. No wonder your chief's been getting all those phone calls."

"I'm not sure how long he can hold out."

"What you mean to say is that we're basically on

our own but maybe with a little help from Enoch Whitehall. I know your boy Heck is tough, but he'll either be forced to give in or be fired in the end."

It wasn't the first time Krystal had been on her own against all odds, but that didn't mean she liked it. "Shit."

"That says it all, and deep shit at that. Do you want to know what I think? I think Dugan Dillon was up to his elbows in whatever George Wakefield is up to. I think it somehow involves the Russians, maybe the FSB or SVR, and that means international espionage. I think Dugan didn't like it one little bit, and I think he planned to bust it wide open. I think he told his wife all about it and told her to pass the info to that Apelbaum character if anything happened to him. I don't know why he chose Apelbaum, maybe because he was the kind of guy who would publish anything to make a splash, even if he had no idea where his information came from. Even with all the mindless crap published these days about the Russians, the Post or Times would at least demand to know who the source was. Despite her watchdog, Katherine Dillon managed to borrow her neighbor's cell phone, and that led to her disappearance and Apelbaum's murder. Paul Dillon is probably scared shitless for the safety of his grandchildren and has been warned not to open his mouth. He's been scared all along, and that's why he's been so uncooperative."

There was no comfort in Strachey's words. It made sense, but it was also worse than she could have imagined that rainy night weeks past when Dugan Dillon's body had been found slumped in his car with his brains blown out. Why were the FBI and the CIA abstaining from involvement when there was every indication that espionage was involved? More than ever she wished she'd taken up Strachey's offer of a drink.

She'd almost forgotten something. "Did I mention that Whitehall and your old friend Harvey Grant have talked about this, specifically about your involvement?"

"Why that sneaky old bastard! He could talk to a feebie but not to me? I suspected as much. Still it's just more confirmation of what I just said. And it makes things even weirder. The more we learn, the more it looks like something both CIA and FBI should be on top of. I don't understand what's holding them back."

"Oh, c'mon, Bob. It's politics pure and simple. Both of those agencies have become highly politicized. Just look at all the leaks to the press."

Strachey shook his head in disgust. "Even so, they're keeping a lid on this. What could be so big, so powerful as to make them back down?"

"Once we know that, we'll have the case solved."

"When the case is solved, I have a feeling it will be only the beginning."

"What do you mean?"

"Consequences. There will be consequences, maybe for us, maybe for a lot of others."

"Whitehall's 'dark stain?'"

His face set and grim, Strachey replied, "I wouldn't be surprised. I think your friend Enoch Whitehall is playing his hand like old J. Edgar would have, *sub rosa* moving the political pieces around the chessboard. And we're his pawns."

CHAPTER 24

She drove slowly back toward her apartment on North Barton Street. It was a long drive from McLean to Arlington, and it gave her time to think.

The sky had clouded over while they were talking, and it had begun to rain. One of the Charger's wipers was worn and smeared the rain across the windshield allowing her only a distorted view of the darkened road ahead. It was an apt metaphor for the Dillon murder case. They were catching glimpses, sketchy outlines of what was really going on, but they needed more, and they needed it fast. They had to do something to bust it open.

If Strachey's speculation was right, Katherine Dillon was the key which meant they had to find her. She tried to avoid the thought that Katherine might already be yet another victim in the string of murders. And what about the two children?

There were at least two people who probably knew where she was: George Wakefield and Paul Dillon. There wasn't a snowball's chance in hell that Wakefield would say anything, but maybe Dugan's father could be persuaded.

Another question was how much longer Chief Heck would be able to back them up. The last thing she wanted was to work without authorization. She'd run that risk once before and nearly been fired as a result. Worse, Ray Velazquez had nearly died. This time she'd convinced a civilian, Strachey, to get involved, and he and Frank Watson both had had to take steps to protect their families. Things would only get worse, and she didn't want to think about how much worse.

When she had suggested that Strachey might want to step back, his face had clouded and he'd said, "Krystal, someone tried to kill me. It's likely they'll keep trying, and I don't intend just to sit around waiting for the next time."

Back at North Barton Street she rushed from the car into the building. The rain was increasing in intensity, and thunder rolled in from a distance beyond the Potomac. With her clothes in a damp pile on the floor, she pulled on an old American University T-shirt and fell into bed. A scotch might calm her enough to get some sleep. She pulled the covers up to her chin and lay there for a long time thinking about that drink before drifting off.

She did not notice the car that stopped in front of her apartment building or the driver who made sure she had retired for the night before driving away.

The rain had stopped by morning leaving traces of ozone in the crystalline air. The leaves on the trees in the small park across the street glistened wetly in the morning light, and puddles had collected in the street. It all reminded her of the calm aftermath of a Mid-Western thunderstorm like those she'd known in Indiana. It had a cleansing effect, and she felt something she'd not felt for a long time – optimism. It was only a small candle in a dark room, but it was there. She decided the clearing sky was a good omen.

By the time she reached the office she'd resolved to pay another visit to Dillon. She filled in Watson on the events of the day before and left him for once speechless. She had to see Chief Heck. She reasoned it was only fair to forewarn him of her plan to talk to Paul Dillon again, but she would not tell him everything. The poor guy had enough on his shoulders already, and there was no telling how he would react to what she'd learned from Enoch Whitehall. Besides, Whitehall had sworn her to secrecy. She reasoned it was OK to share the information with Watson and Strachey – they were members of the team. It wasn't fair to the Chief, she knew, but if heavy artillery began impacting the Arlington County Police she would rather it be directed on her head. The least she could do was provide him with what Strachey would call plausible denial. She wondered what she would do if she were fired.

Heck gave her a wary look when she entered his office and went a shade paler when she told him what she intended to do. "I'm sorry, Chief, but it's the best option for us at this point. I think it's highly likely that he knows where his daughter-in-law is, whether she disappeared of her own free will or whether she was abducted. If she was abducted as we believe, Paul Dillon is a victim of blackmail and keeping quiet to protect her. We think Katherine is the key to wrapping up the case."

The Chief sighed a long sigh and kneaded his temples. "This will trigger another round of threats, you know," he said.

"If our suspicions are right and we can get him to talk, I don't think there will be any calls this time. The idea is to pressure him to cooperate. He won't want to advertise it if he does."

The wary look returned. "Things have calmed down since the last round of angry phone calls and messages," he said. "But our situation is precarious. You know I'm rooting for you, but I have the entire Department to worry about. The barbarians are at the gate, and I don't know how much longer I can fend them off."

He was wavering, but at least he was up front about it.

"Chief, if we come up empty this time, I promise it'll be the last. But we have to give it one more shot."

She felt sorry for Heck and regretted not telling him the whole story, but she'd convinced herself she was doing him a favor.

After an uncomfortable silence, Heck said, "OK, Krystal. But this is the last time."

"You won't regret it, Chief."

"I hope not," he mumbled, "but I have a feeling I will."

Ten minutes later she and Watson were in the Challenger on the way to the Dillon residence out on Route 7.   They followed the George Washington Parkway out past CIA Headquarters to the Beltway before finally catching Route 7 West.   The endless roadwork and construction in the Tyson's Corner area slowed them, and traffic was jammed into alternating single lanes even at mid-morning, a monument to so-called economic development

"I don't think anybody really works anymore," observed Watson. "They just drive around in their cars all day. Where are all these people going?"

"They're searching for new ways to spend their money. Some people aren't happy if they don't buy a new whatzit every day."

"You know, way back Washington had a fine

tram system. The tracks ran all over town down the middle of streets so people didn't have to drive everywhere. They didn't need so many cars. Then a guy named O. Roy Chalk started a bus company and probably paid off enough politicians to tear up the tracks and switch to reliance on the internal combustion engine. And the rest is history."

Krystal gritted her teeth as she navigated through yet another road construction site. "I guess there's a moral there somewhere."

"Remember the Unabomber, Kaczynski? He believed that every advance in technology served technology more than people, that in the end it just leaves everybody running around in circles serving the machines."

She gave him a sidewise glance. "You're sounding philosophical this morning, Frank, and you're scaring me."

He snorted. "Hell, that bastard was right. Just take a look around. Everybody has their nose pointed at a smart phone. Most people live in a virtual world controlled by Silicon Valley. Pretty soon everybody will just be sitting around with virtual reality helmets on their heads pretending they're slaying dragons, or something. And as their minds turn to mush and their asses grow wider their rights will become more and more restricted, but they won't care – they'll be the slaves of a few billionaires who live on their own islands."

"Well, if everybody's at home at least there won't be so much traffic."

Watson guffawed. "Jeez, so there's a bright side to the enslavement of humanity, after all."

"Have you turned into a communist, Frank?"

"Hell no. I'm just an old counry boy, and I can't wait for retirement so I can go back home and live the simple life. I can't tell you how many times I've thought about chucking it up here and moving back south, maybe get a job as a county sheriff or something. It'd be a much better life for the kids."

"Why haven't you done it yet?"

"Well, we have a nice place far enough away from all this concrete to be bearable, and the pay's not too bad. I'd hate to give up my seniority. But in just a couple of years I'll have enough time in to draw a pension, and then I'm outta here."

Krystal had not yet reached the point where she felt a great deal of nostalgia for southern Indiana. "You know, Frank, I spent the first eighteen years of my life plotting an escape from the 'simple life.' I was tired of flat corn and milo fields as far as the eye could see, of little towns that were hollowed out whenever a new Walmart was built and put the locals out of business, and people sinking slowly into poverty. I joined the Army after a stint at community college and got out. I don't miss it, at all."

"Well, you're a lot younger than me, Red. Give it some time."

They picked up speed past Tyson's Corner and were soon passing Leesburg. Shortly thereafter they were on the long driveway leading to the Dillon house.

Again, they'd not called ahead, not even to Dillon's office, taking the chance that he would be at home. If he were not there, they would question his wife.

But Paul Dillon was at home. He opened the

door, and his eyes widened when he saw them. He was dressed in a polo shirt and chinos, and it was clear he'd lost some weight. His formerly well groomed hair had grown shaggy. His face was thinner, and the tan was fading. It looked like he'd not been out of the house since their last visit. "What do you want?" he asked in a toneless voice.

Locking eyes with him, Krystal said, "We need to talk to you about your daughter-in-law and your grandchildren."

Dillon backed away a step and started to close the door, but Watson slapped his hand against it. "I wouldn't do that," he said, his voice a low growl.

Dillon looked surprised and a little scared. "I have nothing to say to you."

"And why is that Mr. Dillon?" asked Krystal. Watson still held the door open, and she took a step closer to the lawyer. "What are you hiding? What are you so afraid of? We know that Katherine was abducted, and not just by any criminal. She was abducted by a foreign intelligence service and is surely in great danger. You need to talk to us before it's too late."

Another figure loomed suddenly behind Dillon, a tall, dark figure with a polished skull. He shoved Dillon aside and forcefully slapped Watson's arm away from the door. The man was instantly recognizable. He was the same hulking black man they'd seen in George Wakefield's office.

"You heard the man," he growled. "Leave now."

Krystal stepped back and looked at him hard. "You just assaulted a police officer, and I'm putting you under arrest. Step out here and put your hands behind your back. Now."

Her hand went to the Beretta on her belt, but the big man was faster. He'd been half concealed behind the door, but now he stepped out, and there was a large pistol in his hand. He must have had it drawn all the time, hiding it behind the lawyer. He pointed the weapon at Krystal, taking his eyes off of Watson who struck like a rattlesnake, grabbing the pistol and forcing it away from Krystal while he chopped at the guy's throat with his other hand.

The weapon discharged harmlessly, the round ricocheting off the portico floor, shattering the tile. Wakefield's man staggered back, but he was too big to fall so easily. His hand went to his throat, making choking sounds, as Krystal drew her Beretta.

Watson had not succeeded in wresting the pistol from the big man's grasp, and he started to raise it again. Krystal fired without hesitation, two quick shots aimed center mass. The powerful .45 ACP slugs should have knocked him down, but he slammed against the door jamb. As his knees buckled he still managed to raise his pistol. Watson had taken a step back and drawn his weapon, as well. He too shot twice, and the man sprawled on his back, now coughing up copious gouts of blood. Still, he'd not dropped his weapon, and Watson stepped in and placed a foot hard on his gun hand.

The wounded man was now making gurgling sounds and his eyes went wide as he struggled to breathe through the blood filling his lungs. He spasmed, his legs jerking straight, and then was still, eyes still open staring at something no one else could see.

Dillon stumbled back into the house and doubled up to vomit on the polished slate floor.

CHAPTER 25

Watson bent over to place two fingers against the neck of their prone assailant and felt no pulse. He stood and shook his head. "He's dead. Are you OK, Red?"

Krystal was shaking as the adrenalin drained from her system. "Yeah. I just need a sec to catch my breath. I sure as hell didn't expect that."

"Good reflexes, though. I'll call for back-up and a wagon." He turned and started for the Challenger.

Paul Dillon had recovered from his shock enough to say, "No. You can't call anybody. If they find out what's happened Katherine and the children will be killed."

She put up a hand to stop Watson and asked Dillon, "Is there anybody else here like this guy?"

Dillon couldn't take his eyes off the body. There were spots of vomit on the front of his shirt and pants. When he didn't respond, Krystal asked again, "Does this guy have a friend somewhere in the house or outside?"

He turned his attention to her with none of the arrogance and condescension he'd showed them before. "No. They switch out every twelve hours." He pointed at the corpse, "This one got here at eight this morning."

"Please go find your wife and wait for us in the living room."

Watson returned to her side. "I think I'd better check around outside the house just in case there's another surprise waiting for us."

"Good idea."

While Watson was checking, Krystal found the Dillons waiting for her in a sunroom at the rear of the house overlooking a large slate patio and a swimming pool. Beyond was pasture land where several horses grazed, oblivious to the drama inside, and beyond that a panorama of mountains.

Mrs. Dillon was sobbing softly, her face buried in his shoulder, and Paul Dillon looked like anything but the calm, powerful figure he had cut in his office. When he looked at Krystal there was desperation in his eyes. "You didn't call anyone, did you?"

The furniture in the sun room was mostly wicker with an abundance of large, colorful cushions. The Dillons were on a love seat with a low, glass-topped table in front, a vase of wilting flowers sitting on it. Krystal chose a chair opposite them.

"No, Mr. Dillon," she said, "We haven't made a call yet, though I'm sure you realize there are measures that must be taken. The body must be removed and official reports filed. As a lawyer you must know that."

"But you can't, at least not now. You just don't understand what's happening."

"Then why don't you tell me, and I advise you not to leave anything out."

The shootout with Wakefield's goon and his resulting death placed a heavy burden on Krystal. Any shooting by a police officer must be reported, and reported promptly. The officer involved would be placed on temporary duty while an internal investigation was conducted. There were forms to fill out, witness statements to take, and a board of inquiry in some instances. Even worse, they were in Fairfax County, which meant the locals would have to be brought in, too. She knew of no official mechanism for keeping the shooting quiet. Her obligation at this instant was to call in a report and wait for the inevitable crowd of responders to arrive. The longer she waited to report, the worse things could become. There was no room in the regulations, or the law for that matter, for individual discretion in such matters.

And there was Frank Watson to consider. His career and the quiet retirement he had planned also would be in jeopardy if she didn't follow the rules.

In the balance was the safety of Katherine Dillon and her children.

The question was: whom could she trust?

A lot would depend on what Paul Dillon was about to say.

Dillon had retrieved some calm, and he stared at her now with equal amounts of fear and speculation. Even *in extremis* the lawyer's calculating mind was turning over alternatives.

"Mr. Dillon," she said, "there's just no more time for you to dither. That body bleeding all over your floor out there proves to me that George Wakefield is holding something over you, controlling you. You've been holding back important information, obstructing justice, in fact. Your own son was viciously murdered, and in all the weeks that followed you've told us exactly nothing that would further our investigation. Now talk, or I'm calling in the troops."

"It's Katherine's fault," he began. "If only she hadn't given information to that blogger ..."

"Your son's death would go unanswered. We know all about that so-called 'nanny.' Her job was to guard Katherine, make sure she did nothing to endanger whatever it was that got Dugan killed. But Katherine was brave and took a chance. And do you know what, Mr. Dillon? I think she was braver and a lot smarter than you. What did you think would happen? Did you really believe that George Wakefield would just wait 'til things blew over and then let you and your family get on with your lives?

Dillon opened his mouth to say something, but she continued talking. "No, Mr. Dillon. That could never have been his plan. The real plan was to keep you silent until a suitable time and method could be worked out to silence you, your wife, your daughter-in-law, and your grandchildren forever. A tragic accident could be arranged, or maybe a suicide or two. No. Wakefield would never set you free."

Dillon buried his face in his hands. "You're right," he mumbled. "But what could I do? They had that vicious woman at Dugan's house. We were helpless."

"You could have said something when we saw you the first time, and we could have taken care of that problem without too much trouble. But you didn't, and two more innocent men died, plus the guy here today. But this isn't getting us anywhere, and time is running out for you to explain what the hell has been going on."

Paul Dillon was a defeated man. "I started working with George Wakefield almost as soon as he set up his security consulting firm, and I assigned Dugan to be the corporate counsel. Things started out slow for George. He wasn't making a lot of money. His reputation was not the greatest, and a lot of people just didn't trust him. But a couple of years ago, things started to pick up when that Russian lawyer showed up. Money started rolling in. I discovered that most of the money was Russian. This worried me somewhat, given the illicit nature of so much that is Russian these days, and I told Dugan to keep a sharp eye out.

"Huge amounts of money were passing through Wakefield's accounts and ending up in shell corporations in various tax havens. George was paying us top dollar, more than we might have expected, and it soon became our most profitable account. We set up office space in our firm for the Russian lawyer."

"This Russian lawyer was the same woman who kidnapped Katherine?"

Dillon hung his head. "Yes. George had Dugan and her set up a series of so-called non-profit political action organizations throughout the country, really just shells with one of George's people heading each one. Then the money started flowing into these non-profits, and from there into the political campaigns of certain politicians. It didn't seem to make a lot of difference to George which political party these politicians belonged to, just how avaricious they were. In the end they became addicted to Wakefield's money, which was really Russian money. Do you get the picture?"

"You're saying that through George Wakefield, the Russians were buying political leverage?" Krystal began to understand why people were trying to shut down the investigation.

"More like blackmail, I think," said Watson. "None of those Congressmen and Senators could afford for it to become public that they'd accepted Russian money, especially during an election year. Dugan's conscience started bothering him, and he insisted George put an end to it. It was highly illegal, and Dugan was young enough still to be idealistic."

"Unlike his father?"

Dillon lowered his head again. "Unlike his father," he repeated in a dull voice. "Past a certain point, scruples in Washington become pliable. A lot of that money was coming into our firm. We would be ruined too if the truth came out. And who cares about a few more crooked politicians, anyway?" Dillon's voice now acquired a bitter edge. "But Dugan didn't care, didn't care that he could destroy what I'd built up over the years."

Krystal was repelled by the creature before her. "So your son had to be eliminated."

There was a flash of anger from Dillon. "I had nothing to do with that. What kind of man do you think I am? Wakefield somehow gulled Dugan to the club and had him killed. He has a lot of shadowy characters working for him, mostly former intel and military - guns for hire. I'm sure he had one of them do it. I don't think it ever entered Dugan's head what a dangerous game he was playing."

"How did Wakefield find out what Dugan was thinking."

Again, Dillon lowered his head. "I told him. I promised to take the account away from Dugan and send him somewhere far away from Washington. I promised to handle any blowback and pointed out that anything Dugan knew was subject to attorney-client privilege. And George said he was OK with that."

"But he wasn't."

"Obviously not. Oh, he made a great show of sympathy after Dugan was killed, but he made sure I knew he was still concerned, especially because we didn't know how much Dugan had confided in Katherine."

"And the Russian spook was in Katherine's house even before we arrived to inform her of her husband's death."

It had all been pre-arranged. The "nanny" had in all likelihood appeared on Katherine Dillon's doorstep at the same time Dugan was being murdered. George Wakefield had orchestrated the macabre dance just as he would have planned an intricate intelligence operation for the CIA. He left nothing to chance. And he undoubtedly had something deadly in mind for Katherine, as well. But it had gone awry, and things had gotten complicated.

"What do we do now, Red?" Watson had entered the room in time to catch the last part of the conversation.

Still debating her next step, Krystal asked, "Do you know where Wakefield is holding Katherine and the kids?"

"We have a summer house up in St. Michaels. That's where they went ... with that Russian woman. And I'm sure Wakefield has others watching them."

"You're sure the dead guy's relief won't show up until eight tonight?"

"That's the way it's worked from the beginning of this nightmare," replied Dillon.

She rose to her feet. "You two stay here and don't move. I need to talk to my partner."

There were sliding glass doors leading out onto a broad terrace. She and Watson stepped outside and closed the doors behind them.

"This is getting hairy, Frank. I just don't see how we can handle it alone."

"I agree."

"Any ideas?"

"We could call Strachey."

"That's only one more person, and he has less authority than we do. I don't think we can risk an assault on Dillon's summer house with so few. Damn."

"Enoch Whitehall?"

"Maybe, but he made it clear this is something not to be discussed on the phone. It would take too much time to arrange a meeting with him. We only have until eight tonight at the best."

Watson scratched his head. "You know, I still can't understand why the FBI hasn't been all over this. We have murder, kidnapping, and espionage, at least a sort of espionage."

"I don't either, but Whitehall said the FBI is hands off."

She couldn't shake the conviction that Whitehall was using her as a pawn, someone to stir the pot and maybe bring something to the surface that would justify action on his part.

She had an idea.

"I'm going to call Strachey."

"But you said ..."

"I know. But we need his spooky brain, and I

think there's something he can do. But he's got to do it fast."

She punched Strachey's number into her cell. When he answered she told him where they were and that he should get there pronto.

It was an agonizing thirty-five minutes before Strachey's BMW drew up in front of the Dillon house. It was nearly noon. Eight hours before their self-imposed deadline for action.

It was hard to miss the dead man sprawled at the door. It took another fifteen minutes to fill him in on what had happened and what Paul Dillon had said.

"I don't like the odds, guys," said Strachey. "I've done something similar before, and it was definitely no fun, even with automatic weapons and body armor. We're going to need help. And if we're going up against trained military types, I mean the armed to the teeth kind of help."

"But there might be only the woman holding them out there," suggested Watson.

"I'm not so sure," said Krystal. "Remember what Dillon said about the kind of men Wakefield has with him."

"If I were Wakefield," said Strachey, "I'd have a couple of men outside guarding the perimeter. He's not the kind of man who would leave anything to chance."

"I can think of only one place to go," said Krystal. "Enoch Whitehall." She was thinking of her get out of jail free card.

Strachey chewed on this for a beat or two. He still had a trace of the old CIA animus for the FBI. "What do you think he can do? He wasn't particularly forthcoming when you saw him."

"There's no one else with the authority to pull together an operation quick enough," she said. "With so many different jurisdictions involved, the cops would spend all their time arguing. And there's the little matter of the corpse here that would take Frank and me out of the picture entirely. I intend to see this through to the end."

"So what do you suggest?"

"I want you to go see Whitehall while Frank and I head out to St. Michaels and reconnoiter the house."

"What makes you think Whitehall will agree to talk to me?"

"I'll set up the meeting, and I know I can trust you to brief Whitehall accurately. You have experience in this sort of thing." She wanted to keep Strachey out of the line of fire when the questioning began.

Strachey shot a glance toward the house. "What about the Dillons? You're going to leave them alone with a corpse at their door?"

"They're just going to have to tough it out until tonight," she said. "If they'd been half as brave as Katherine this would have been over a long time ago."

"If Paul Dillon had been an honest man, it wouldn't have happened in the first place, and his son would still be alive."

"And if Whitehall does nothing?"

"Then we think of something else."

CHAPTER 26

George Wakefield smoked a long Cuban cigar as he surveyed his domain from behind his desk. The panelled walls filled with pictures of himself with various foreign leaders and guerilla fighters, the huge bookcase that displayed the spines of thick, leather-bound volumes he had never read. There was the occasional framed newspaper story with him as the subject. It was all his, and there was no phalanx of Langley seventh floor lawyers to tell him what he could and could not do.

In fact, he'd become bigger than Langley. Seen to its logical conclusion, his project would place in his hands more power and influence than any of the *chupatintas*, bureaucrats, in any of the alabaster halls of Washington. All he'd needed was an ally with unlimited funds, and he'd found such a person in Moscow. Of course, the Kremlin and Russian Intelligence were involved, but they were far away. Washington would be his fiefdom.

He admired the new Russians. They were men who thought as he thought, who enjoyed power and were ruthless enough to use it to reach their own ends. He told himself he was working WITH them, not FOR them. They were partners in a joint endeavor.

His revery was interrupted by the ring of a cell phone in his desk drawer, one of the many untraceable throwaways he used to communicate with a certain number of his employees, the ones entrusted with special tasks. He withdrew the phone and put it to his ear. The caller was the man he'd assigned to keep track of the nosy female detective and her dimwit sidekick.

"Boss, something's going on. I followed the two cops out to the Dillon place, and they were in there for over an hour, and then that guy Strachey showed up."

"Did they see you?"

"I'm pretty sure they didn't. The cops have no idea they're being tailed."

The night before, the woman had been observed entering an address in D.C., and then she'd driven all the way out to Robert Strachey's house in McLean. A check of the tax records showed that the house in D.C. belonged to a private foundation based in San Antonio, Texas. He'd never heard of it. His surveillant had reported that the woman had been dressed up for the visit. Maybe she'd gone to a party of some kind. But any meeting with Strachey sent up a flare. He'd pulled surveillance off the ex-CIA operative after the failed hit and run. Strachey was, after all, a professional and it would serve Wakefield better to let things cool down before making another attempt. But now he was at Paul Dillon's house with the nosy cops.

"What's going on now?"

"Wait a minute." The surveillant's voice was excited. "Two cars are driving out. The two cops are leaving, and so is Strachey."

Wakefield wished he'd assigned more than one man to follow the cops. "Follow the cops. See where they're going. I'll call Delron. He's on duty at the house now."

"I'm on my way, Mr. Wakefield."

Wakefield grabbed another burner phone from the drawer and punched the speed dial. No answer.

Something was wrong. He decided to send a pair of men to the Dillon house. It would take them a while to get there, but he needed to know what was going on.

Ninety minutes later the surveillant on the cops reported that they had taken the Route 50 exit off the Beltway and were now heading East into Maryland.

His contentment evaporated. The cops were heading for St. Michaels, and that meant Paul Dillon had told them where the hostages were being held. He cursed the lawyer.

What had happened to his man Delron? His men would report soon.

CHAPTER 27

Tension and heavy traffic combined to make the long drive into the District of Columbia torturous for Robert Strachey. The task of convincing a high-ranking FBI official to do something he might not like and the desperation behind it bore down on him, making his limbs feel heavy and useless.

This wasn't his first visit to FBI Headquarters to meet Enoch Whitehall. The ageless "man in black" knew a great deal about him, including a few things Strachey would have preferred he did not know. Whitehall had an almost supernatural ability to find things out, but he also knew how to keep a secret, for which Strachey was grateful.

He found a parking place on the National Mall and walked the remaining two blocks to the crumbling edifice of the Hoover Building at 935 Pennsylvania Avenue. At the entrance a uniformed guard confirmed his name was on the visitors list and handed him a plastic card with "visitor – escort required" in big red letters that he clipped to his jacket pocket.

A crewcut young man in a neat, dark suit led him to an elevator, and a few minutes later they stopped at their destination on the third floor. A plaque at the side of the door announced that the territory beyond was the doman of Executive Assistant Director for Counter Intelligence, Enoch Whitehall.

The escort knocked and opened the door. They entered an outer office dominated by a stern looking woman of indeterminate age who was Whitehall's secretary/receptionist. Krystal had dubbed her "the dragon guarding the gate." The only other thing she knew was that her name was Jeanne.

The dragon dismissed the escort and instructed Watson to one of a set of straight-backed wooden chairs against the wall. "Director Whitehall will be with you shortly," she said.

Not even Murphy knew much about Whitehall himself beyond his official position and the fact that he seemed to have been with the FBI forever.

The intercom on the dragon's desk buzzed, and she said, "You may go in now." She pointed to a solid oak door in the wall behind her desk.

Strachey walked to the door and stood there feeling awkward, composing what he would say. The dragon said, "Just open the door and go in. He doesn't bite ... most of the time."

He braced himself and opened the door. Whitehall was standing looking out a window overlooking Pennsylvania Avenue. His tall, spare figure was slightly hunched, and his aquiline nose was prominent in profile, like a bird of prey. He gave the impression of a man from another time.

Whitehall turned and stepped toward him, hand outstretched. "Mr. Strachey," he said. "we meet again. And you are here on behalf of Krystal Murphy?"

"Yes, I am."

The FBI man's face was narrow with high cheekbones and gray eyes under shaggy brows. His graying hair was parted on one side and combed in a simple, no nonsense style that evoked the early twentieth century. A charcoal gray suit hung from his frame. His grasp was firm and dry.

"Let's sit over at the conference table."

Whitehall spoke in a quiet voice that was neither high nor low at a pitch barely above the ambient noise of the room and arid as a desert breeze. There was no way to know if this was natural or a means of insuring the close attention of his interlocutors.

The office hadn't changed since his last visit – austere to the point of being spartan and very nearly anonymous. The heavy government issue furniture, leather sofa and chairs, wooden table and desk, were from a by-gone era. Such furniture had been switched out all over Washington over forty years ago, but not in this office. The only picture on the walls was one of a younger Whitehall shaking hands with J. Edgar Hoover. Aside from that there was only a flat-screen TV and a whiteboard.

The round conference table in one corner was sufficient to seat six comfortably in leather upholstered wooden chairs. Whitehall chose a seat opposite Strachey. "I instructed Krystal to contact me only in case of extreme urgency. What has happened?"

Strachey began his recitation of the morning's events at Paul Dillon's house. He was nervous at first but gained more confidence as the narrative proceeded. Whitehall listened in silence, his expression unreadable.

"... so you see, sir, you're the only person we could bring this to."

"And you say Krystal and Officer Watson are on their way to St. Michaels now?"

"Yes. "

Whitehall was silent for several beats. His expression did not change, but the gray eyes seemed to grow in intensity as he stared hard at Strachey.

Finally, he asked, "What do you think I can do?"

The question might be a positive sign. "Three things. First, we need everything placed under FBI authority. There are just too many jurisdictions involved, and there's no time to organize a joint operation among at least three different police departments in two states. Second, send a couple of your people to the Dillon house right away to take charge of the crime scene, watch over the Dillons in case another of Wakefield's thugs shows up. Third, we need back-up to take the house in St. Michaels. We don't know how much opposition we'll run into out there."

"It's not as easy as you might imagine." The FBI man's eyes were still locked with Strachey's. "There is very little time, and I would guess that Krystal and Watson already are over half-way to St. Michaels by now?"

Strachey checked his Rolex and nodded. "They're not going to do anything rash. They won't go in with guns blazing. The plan is to case the house and then decide how to go about it, or turn it over the the FBI. But regardless, they'll wait until dark before doing anything. That gives you a lot of time."

Enoch Whitehall was in an uncharacteristic bind. The directors of National Intelligence, the CIA, and the FBI were in accord on one thing: the activities of Paul Wakefield and his allies were radioactive, so much so that they were not to be touched. If something blew up with regard to Wakefield, the ripples would spread across Washington and beyond leaving chaos in their wake. At least that was the common opinion.

But the men heading America's intelligence and law enforcement agencies had become political, biased, and this went very much against Enoch Whitehall's nature. His view of the world was much more black and white than gray. Certainly, politics had always played a role in FBI operations, most egregiously during the long reign of J. Edgar Hoover. But the welfare of the nation was not something to be politicized. The people of this country were not so weak as to abandon all hope at the first sign of trouble.

The powers that be were dithering, hoping against hope that the situation could be controlled quietly and that with time the ship of state would right itself. Enoch Whitehall did not believe letting events follow their course would necessarily provide anodyne results.

And in this instance, four people had died violent deaths, maybe more, there was evidence of blackmail, and an abduction had taken place. Lives, two of them children, were in the balance, and the only ones seeking justice against all odds were Krystal Murphy, Robert Strachey, and Watson. Yes, he had given a clue to Murphy and gently prodded her to continue her investigation. But there was no way he could have anticipated the events at the Dillon home or Murphy's rash action. In retrospect, he should not have been surprised by her impetuosity. Whatever happened now would be at least in part his responsibility.

Any action Whitehall might take on his own authority could be, almost certainly would be, career ending. The FBI had been his life for more decades than he cared to remember. He'd fought crime and he'd fought espionage and was fortunate to have had more victories than defeats. He sought no glory. He had no ambitions beyond his own office, a quality appreciated by succeeding directors. He'd hoped to remain where he was until he died, preferably behind his desk.

The FBI man shook his head and sighed. "Well, Strachey, your friend, Krystal, has a way of making things happen, and now she's forcing the issue. The problem is that she can't begin to imagine the consequences."

Strachey started to protest, but Whitehall silenced him with a wave of his hand. "There is, in fact, no way she possibly could imagine the consequences."

"With all due respect, sir, I need an answer from you. If there's nothing you can do, I'll just be heading out to St. Michaels."

Despite Washington, D.C. prohibitions, he had his pistol in his car and an AR-15 in the trunk with plenty of ammunition. If all else failed, he could easily be in St. Michaels before dark.

CHAPTER 28

It was not entirely unexpected that Krystal and Frank did not detect that they were being followed. George Wakefield employed professionals, after all, but more than that, it is the nature of police to be on the other end of surveillance in order to apprehend criminals. It would be highly irregular to the point of rare for someone to be stalking them. Spies like Robert Strachey, on the other hand, are usually engaged in what might truthfully be termed "criminal" activity and thus must be extremely sensitive to the possibility of surveillance. They've made an entire science of it.

The distance from the Dillon house to St. Michaels, a prosperous and picturesque village on the Chesapeake Bay in Maryland, is a little over 100 miles. Heavy traffic, construction and tolls along Route 50 East meant it would take considerably more than two hours to traverse the distance.

Paul Dillon had drawn a rough sketch of the floor plans of his house on one of the bay's inlets.

"Don't call anyone, and don't leave the house," were Krystal's final instructions to the Dillons. Someone will be here soon to take charge of the situation."

She hoped they would heed her words.

Krystal was driving, and Watson asked from the passenger seat, "How do you think Strachey will do with Whitehall?"

"He'll do alright. They speak the same

language."

Watson had never been to FBI Headquarters despite his long service in the area. He'd attended a couple of training courses at Quantico. The one on forensics had been particularly interesting. The one on "processing stress and enhancing performance with yoga" had provided an opportunity to sleep, a perfectly acceptable alternative to yoga in Watson's view.

"I surely hope so," said Watson, "They have some strange ideas."

Krystal cursed the road construction and the long lines at the toll booths.

Ironically enough, Watson had the radio tuned to his favorite country music station, and Carrie Underwood was belting out "Jesus Take The Wheel."

Past Annapolis, traffic sped up, and they soon were on the Bay Bridge across the Chesapeake. After crossing Kent Narrows the scenery became rural, and Route 50 carried them through small towns, finally curving southward until they at last turned back westward at Easton and caught Route 33 that would take them into St. Michaels.

St. Michaels sits on a narrow strip of land that juts into the Eastern Bay, first heading northwest and then abruptly turning south toward Tilghman Island. The Dillon and Wakefield houses were on the waterfront lots on an inlet north of Hambleton Island.

There was not a doubt in George Wakefield's mind. The two cops were on their way to St. Michaels. Their destination was confirmed as soon as they headed south on Route 50. The fact that they were alone gave him some confidence that he could contain the situation. He instructed his man to suspend the surveillance. As long as they thought they were undetected, Wakefield had the advantage.

He called for his driver. Time for him to leave for St. Michaels. The cops had not shown him proper respect, and he looked forward to questioning them. He could answer all their questions now, but it would do them no good.

The Rubicon would have been crossed, and he could not risk setting them free. Exactly how to dispose of them would be complicated. He needed to turn his mind to something imaginative, perhaps a car wreck somewhere far from St. Michaels.

The men he'd sent to check the Dillon house reported finding Delron's body and the two Dillons alone. Strangely, there were no police. This puzzled Wakefield, but he took it as a sign his luck was still holding and gave them instructions to take the couple to St. Michaels.

He was angry at Paul Dillon. Maybe a murder suicide scenario would work there. The older couple, distraught at the loss of their only son couldn't bear to go on living. Yes, that could be arranged.

Leaving the car behind, Krystal and Watson approached the Dillon house on foot from the south through a large, wooded lot. There were three houses fronting on the inlet, separated from one another by thick growths of trees. Dillon's house was on the center lot. A boat was moored to a dock.

It was still several hours before the sun would

set, and Krystal didn't want to get too close without cover of darkness. A quick reconnoiter from the cover of the woods would suffice for now.

A long, narrow gravelled road led from the main road for several hundred feet through the woods to the house, ending in a paved, circular drive where two cars were parked. One of them was Katherine Dillon's SUV. There was no sign of life.

Watson stayed in the trees to the south, crawling as close to the house as possible without being seen, while Krystal circled toward the water. The trees grew quite close to the house there, and she crept as near as she dared. She was debating whether to risk a peek in a window or wait until dark when she heard a shout that ended abruptly. It was Watson's voice, she was sure.

She drew her pistol and made her way back toward where they had split up, cursing silently all the way. Things were going sideways before they even had a chance to assess the situation. The best guess was that Frank had run into a guard, and from the way his shout had been cut off mid-voice, the guard had gotten the best of him.

These fears were confirmed a moment later when a male voice called from the direction of the house. "Hey, Murphy, we know you're out there. Show yourself or your flunkie here gets a bullet in the brain."

She cautiously approached the tree line until she could see Watson, his knees buckled, supported between two large men dressed in black tactical clothing, and another equally large man looking expectantly toward the woods. He held an AR-15 and looked like someone who knew how to use it.

She lay in a dark spot and waited to see what happened.

Again, the man shouted, "Murphy, we don't care whether this piece of shit lives or dies. It's you the boss wants to have a talk with. We know you're there, and we have a half-dozen of our friends behind you now. It's only a matter of time, so stop wasting ours."

He placed the muzzle of his rifle against Frank's head, which hung on his chest suggesting he was unconscious, or maybe already dead. How the hell had they been discovered? This had all the earmarks of an ambush. Her first thought was that Paul Dillon had warned Wakefield, and she felt a blazing anger toward the lawyer.

Now Watson's captor racked a round into the chamber of his rifle. "Are you ready to see him die?" he shouted.

Why had she done this? It had been a gamble from the start. What difference did it make, really, whether or not Dugan Dillon's murder was solved? If she'd been in her right mind, she would have called in the shooting that morning and let events take their course. Why had she been so eager to risk everything on her instincts alone? Her stubborn persistence had probably gotten herself and Frank Watson killed.

She holstered her weapon, took a deep breath, and rose to her feet. "I'm here," she shouted. "I'm coming out." She raised her hands and stepped out of the tree line.

"Lock your fingers behind your head and walk ... slowly ... to us." The goon now had his rifle pointed at her.

She obeyed, and as she stepped forward more men in black tactical gear emerged from the woods and pointed their weapons at her. The goon hadn't been lying. And these guys were good, really good. She and Watson had seen nothing to arouse suspicion during their approach.

She halted in front of Frank's captors. They were all cut from the same fabric, tough guys with calm eyes devoid of anger or any other emotion, like men doing a familiar job. Their confident control of the weapons signaled experienced fighters. She and Frank wouldn't have stood a chance against them in a gunfight.

One of the men slung his weapon over his shoulder and approached her from behind. He disarmed her and pulled her arms behind her back where he secured them with plastic zip cuffs. Then he patted her down as she locked eyes with the leader. The pat-down was thoroughly professional and spared no part of her body, but she refused to flinch.

Nearer now, she saw blood streaming down Watson's face. He was beginning to regain consciousness and struggled feebly in their grasp, but his hands already had been secured behind his back. One of the men delivered a vicious kick to the back of his knee that caused him to tumble to the ground where the second man slashed the toe of a boot several times into his mid-section.

Krystal tried to step forward but was held back by the man behind her. "You don't have to do that," she shouted.

The leader said, "That's enough, Billy. He won't give us any trouble. Pick him up." Turning to Krystal he said, "We can do anything we damn well like any time we want. And don't forget; your boyfriend here is expendable." There was no anger in his voice, just the calm, menacing words of a man in total control of the situation.

Two of them lifted a groaning, only half-conscious Watson by the elbows and started dragging him toward the house. The leader instructed Krystal to follow, and the rest fell in behind, a triumphant hunting party returning to camp with their prey.

The large house had two wings, one smaller than the other which was probably intended as guest quarters. Krystal and Watson were deposited in a bedroom. They tossed Frank onto the bed and placed another zip tie around his ankles. He continued to moan softly, and his face was white under the blood.

Krystal was placed on a straight-backed wooden chair. They secured her feet and then bound her tightly to the chair with a length of rope.

One of the dark-clad goons remained with them and took a chair by the door. He was one of the bearded ones.

"What do you intend to do with us?" she asked.

He regarded her balefully for a few beats, debating whether to answer. Finally, "Whatever Wakefield says."

She didn't want to think about what Wakefield had in store for them. "Are Katherine Dillon and her children safe?"

The guard didn't answer.

CHAPTER 29

George Wakefield liked an audience. Nothing felt better than being the center of attention. This personality trait accounted in large part for his unorthodox operating style when he was still with the CIA. Some admired him, more hated him, but it made no difference.

The Seventh Floor frowned at him a lot of the time, but he was safe as long as he was successful. In the end, when risky operations went out of vogue, it was the lawyers that forced him out - limp-wristed, mealy-mouthed slugs who had made risk-aversion the guiding tenet of the Agency. And when they started putting analysts in charge of operations he knew it was time to get out. He was still only in his mid-fifties, and it was high time to leave.

His years in intelligence operations, especially the sort of operations in which he engaged, had dulled any sense of right and wrong. The operation was the thing, and all that counted was success. He'd never killed anyone personally, but he did not hesitate to order others to mete out death.

The Russian approach was much more akin to his preferred personal style than the CIA's. Russians were ruthless in achieving their goals, especially the new guys running the show over there. In fact, Wakefield felt much more comfortable with them than he ever had at the CIA.

Sitting in the rear of the Lincoln Towncar as it sped toward the Eastern Shore, he considered how to approach the immediate problem. The cops, of course, would have to disappear in the end. That would leave the ex-CIA guy, Robert Strachey. He knew all about Strachey whose reputation had grown to gargantuan proportions after that operation in Spain.[1] Some went so far as to say he had saved all of Western Europe from nuclear disaster. His sudden resignation had surprised everyone. Wakefield ascribed it to money. Strachey must be making money hand over fist as a 'K' Street lobbyist. Hell, he thought, they were in the same business – peddling influence, buying votes.

He did not understand how the cops had recruited Strachey to work with them, but the man had been asking dangerous questions around Washington. The first attempt on his life had failed, and he remained a loose end that would have to be taken care of before too much time had passed.

Finally, there were the Dillons: Paul and his wife, Katherine and her children. Did he still need them? Up until now he'd believed that as long as Katherine was under his control, the elder Dillon could be counted on to cooperate. But now Wakefield would have to re-think that arrangement.

Watson was not in good shape. He'd regained consciousness but was in obvious pain. Krystal asked the guard, "Can't you do something to help him? At least wipe the blood off."

The guard remained stolidly silent. But he

---

[1] "Retribution," Michael R. Davidson, 2014

didn't object when she spoke to Watson. "Frank, are you OK?"

The words sounded stupid as soon as they were out of her mouth. Of course, he wasn't OK.

"I think my rib's broken, and my head hurts like hell. What happened?" He spoke through clenched teeth.

"I'm an idiot – that's what happened. Wakefield must have known we were coming, and we got ambushed. They knocked you out. We didn't have a chance."

"Why aren't we dead?"

"Damned if I know. I guess Wakefield wants a chat."

"Wunnerful. Katherine and the kids?"

"I don't know. I haven't seen them."

"Not good." He tried to sit up as though he hadn't yet realized he was tied up. "Shee-it."

"Try to rest. Put your head back on the pillow. There's nothing we can do right now."

By the time another hour had passed night had fallen. Krystal's hands and feet were losing their feeling. She could only imagine how uncomfortable poor Frank was. "Can you loosen these cuffs a little? They're stopping my circulation, probably his, too."

Watson said, "Yeah, mine, too."

"Nothing I can do for you," said the guard. He'd been sitting by the door not moving a muscle.

Just as she was about to object, the door opened and the man who'd been giving orders entered. "Time to move," he said to the guard. Untie their feet."

The man giving the orders jerked Krystal up, but she could feel nothing in her feet by now, and she collapsed back onto the chair. "Let me get some circulation restored, or you'll have to carry me out of here," she said, stomping her feet on floor. She felt the familiar pins and needles as feeling returned and was at last able to stand.

It was harder for Frank Watson. Not only had his limbs gone numb, but he still had a splitting headache and a sharp pain in his side where a rib had been broken. He grunted as the guard set him on his feet. "What's going on?" he asked.

The goon giving orders said, "Mr. Wakefield wants to have a talk with you."

He grabbed Krystal's arm tightly and led her out the door. The other one did the same with Watson. They were taken to the central area, a spacious room with a native stone fireplace fit to roast an ox, and comfortable furniture. George Wakefield was lounging in a wingback chair and eyed them with curiousity as they entered.

Katherine Dillon was in a chair against the wall, nervous and twisting her hands in her lap. She stared at Krystal with a mixture of hope and desperation. Next to her were Paul and Nancy Dillon. Paul had his face buried in his hands, and Nancy sobbed softly.

The guards pushed them down side by side on a sofa facing Wakefield. "Which one of you killed Delron?" he asked.

"I did," said Watson

"We both shot the bastard," said Krystal.

Wakefield lit a long cigar. "But you don't seem to have called in the police," he said between puffs. He examined the tip of the cheroot to make sure it was burning evenly. "Why not?"

Neither of them answered.

"Do you know what I think?" said Wakefield, exhaling a thick cloud of blue smoke. "I think you're acting alone. I think you went rogue. But to make sure there are no entanglements with the local cops, I had the body removed and the Dillons brought to this little reunion. So even if the police do show up eventually, they'll find nothing."

She should have called for back-up at the Dillon place immediately and taken the consequences. But second-guessing her decisions would do them no good now.

Her expression must have betrayed her emotions because Wakefield's next words were, "So, you're beaten, Detective." He pronounced the word with disdain. "You're just a tiny cog in a big, inefficient machine, and you bet wrong. I've checked you out, you know. You've been lucky in the past, very lucky, but your luck's run out now, and you and your sidekick here will suffer the consequences of your foolishness."

Upstairs, Mirasol Klyastikova was on her cell phone. Events were unfolding fast, and it was her duty to report to her superiors. George Wakefield was a useful tool, but he was headstrong. He should take no action at this juncture without checking with her principals. But he had ignored her advice, dismissing her suggestion as unnecessary.

Long service in Russian Intelligence had taught Klyastnikova the value of discipline, especially when conducting illegal operations. Discipline had never failed her in the past, and she refused to abandon it now regardless of Wakefield's hubris. Uncoordinated action could bring the entire project crashing down. The former CIA man was too egotistical to realize that she had not been assigned to him for his convenience – her job was to watch him and report his activities. There were too many variables to take the chance of leaving everything up to Wakefield.

She listened carefully to the instructions from the person she had called. When they finished, she locked the two Dillon children in their room and quietly made her way down the rear stairs and out of the house. She understood the reason for the instructions: her superiors did not want a Russian presence in the house at this time.

She knew where the perimeter guards were positioned, so it was not difficult for her to enter the woods and head for the main road where a car would be sent to pick her up and get her out of the area.

George Wakefield was feeling victorious and expansive. "You should have taken the hint, Detective, when your boss received all those complaints about you. A person with any sense at all would have realized it was time to back off. But you didn't. Instead you went rogue and meddled in things bigger and more important than you can imagine."

"Such as you being a Russian agent?" Despite the situation Krystal was curious.

Wakefield laughed derisively. "Agent? I'm not anyone's agent. I'm in charge, the spider at the center of the web sensitive to every vibration. This is the best operation I've ever run. I'm in charge."

"So the Russians are working for you?" She wanted to goad him, keep him talking. She recognized a megalomaniac when she saw one, and that was exactly what George Wakefield was. The longer he talked, the longer they would stay alive.

"In a way," he said, exhaling more blue smoke. "Pretty soon I'll be running this country, and it wasn't so hard to arrange. Do you remember that remark by James Carville about dragging a hundred dollar bill through a trailer park? He said, 'Drag a hundred dollar bill through a trailer park, you never know what you'll find.' Well, it's just the same if you drag a few thousand dollar bills through Congress. Pretty soon those senators and congressmen are eating out of your hand, from both sides of the aisle. They become your puppets. All you have to do is pull the strings. And the way it is these days with the numbers, all you have to do is control a half-dozen or so of them, and you can gum up the works pretty effectively."

"I don't believe you," she said. "They're not that stupid."

He laughed again. "Oh, yes they are, at least enough of them to make a difference. Their average net worth is around fourteen million dollars. Now, how do you think they accumulate all that wealth on government salaries? Do you think they're all altruistic angels? Hell, politicians are the same all over the world. It's just that some of them aren't clever about it. They're all whores, and they all have their price. Get them hooked on the money you give them and they're yours. Inform them that the money they've been taking is illegal, coming from Russia, and they're doubly yours."

Enoch Whitehall's words about a dark stain spreading over Washington now made sense. This must have been what he meant. Whitehall, and probably Strachey's friend Harvey Grant knew what was happening. But nothing was being done. How could that be? All she could do was stare at Wakefield in disgust.

The man's head was wreathed in cigar smoke and his face was contorted in a rictal grin, his green eyes glistening in the reflected light. It was this demonic image of Wakefield that Krystal would always remember.

CHAPTER 30

Their captor's smug words stung Frank Watson more than the pain in his side. "You're lower than a snake's belly, mister, low down and a traitor."

Wakefield regarded him with a sour downturn of his mouth. "Traitor? The value of patriotism is highly exaggerated. It's a simple matter of geography, isn't it? But a man can rise above the random accident of where he was born to achieve the only things that really count – power and wealth. Whoever ends up with the most marbles wins. For example, in the present situation, I'm the winner because I have more power and influence than you. That's why you and your friend ended up isolated and irrelevant. Pathetic. And that's all you need to know." He gestured to the guards. "Pick 'em up. It's time to go."

His men would take the two cops and their car to a remote location in Virginia where a fatal automobile accident would be staged.

The guards, as expressionless as automatons moved toward Krystal and Frank.

Several things happened in quick succession. First, the man who had been standing over Katherine Dillon looked surprised as his chest blossomed red, and he crumpled to the floor. There was a crash of glass and a loud explosion accompanied by blinding light that filled the room. More crashes as doors and windows were smashed and dark-clad figures charged inside. The guards moving toward Krystal and Watson fell next, their weapons clattering to the floor. But Krystal had heard no gunshots.

Sight returned before hearing. Wakefield had not moved, but now he stood, his eyes wildly seeking a way to escape. When he stood and took a step she stuck a leg out, and he tripped over it, sprawling face down on the floor. Her hands were still tied behind her back, but she stood, gauged the distance, and drove the toe of her shoe as hard as she could directly between Wakefield's legs. She was rewarded by a keening howl that hardly sounded like it came from a man. Wakefield rolled on his side and brought his knees up into a fetal position. His face had paled, and tears streamed from his eyes.

CHAPTER 31

The letters "FBI" emblazoned in big, yellow letters on the deep blue uniforms of their rescuers advertised their origin. Krystal was sure they were the Bureau's Hostage Rescue Team out of Quantico. The agent in charge confirmed her conjecture as he cut through the plastic ties on her hands. The team's medic was already tending to Frank Watson, and had stripped off his shirt to reveal an ugly purple welt on his side. The medic bandaged his midsection tightly and said he wanted to get Frank to a hospital for x-rays and to suture his head wound.

"We'll take him to Quantico with the others," said the AIC. "It won't take long, and we have everything necessary there."

As soon as she was released Katherine Dillon ran upstairs where she found her two young children crying but safe, locked in a bedroom. A search of the house and grounds did not turn up the Russian woman.

Krystal's wrists were chafed and red where they had been bound, and she rubbed them to restore circulation. Watson was now lying on the couch, and she knelt beside him. "How are you doing, partner?"

"I've felt better. Where's that SOB, Wakefield?"

"They have him cuffed in the dining room."

"I thought I heard him scream when the fun began. Was he shot?"

"Better. I kicked him in the balls."

Watson rewarded her with a wicked grin. "Almost better than shooting him."

The AIC was a wiry man and without his balaclava appeared to be in his mid-forties with a face that was all sharp angles. He told them the team had two Blackhawk helicopters in the open field at the end of the peninsula. They'd waited for darkness before coming in low, skimming over the water, the muffled blades of the choppers making their approach nearly silent. Wakefield's perimeter guards had all been killed or captured before the assault on the house.

While preparations for their departure were being made Krystal stepped into the dining room where George Wakefield was sitting uncomfortably with his hands cuffed behind his back. He was still pale underneath his tan, but there was defiance in his eyes.

He looked up at her entrance, an ugly sneer on his face. "Don't think you've won, Detective. You have no idea the pressure I can bring to bear. I'll be a free man by tomorrow, and all it will take will be a couple of phone calls to the right people - people I own. You've wasted your time."

A voice sounded behind Krystal, "I don't think so, George." It was Robert Strachey.

It pleased Krystal to see a familiar face. "Bob, when did you get here?"

Just a few minutes ago. The feebies gave me a lift from Washington. We have a couple of SUV's out front. Your friend Whitehall made sure the HRT would let me pass. Are you OK? I saw poor Frank in the other room."

"I'm OK, just a little tired. I can't believe it's over."

Wakefield was regaining his composure. "But

Michael R. Davidson

it's not over, Detective. It's not over by a long shot."

"George," said Strachey, "you're a fucking disgrace to everything the Agency stands for. As far as I'm concerned, they ought to hang you. But not before they sweat you for all you know. Then there'll be a quiet trial, and you'll be heading to a maximum security cell for the rest of your miserable life. No more cigars, no more booze, no more women, no more anything. You'll probably be stark raving mad in the end."

"Bullshit," spat Wakefield, his old swagger returning. "Don't kid yourself. And fuck the Agency and all who sail with her."

A long time ago over a mostly consumed bottle of locally brewed *poitin* and in a philosophical mood a friend in Ireland had advised Strachey that trust and cynicism were opposite sides of the same coin in intelligence work. In Wakefield's case, cynicism had clearly won out. Taut with anger, Strachey invited Krystal to go out and keep Frank company. Another second in Wakefield's company, and he would attempt to strangle the bastard.

"Let's have lunch at the Metropolitan Club next week, Bob," taunted Wakefield to their backs. "My treat. Bring the redhead, too. We'll have a few laughs."

Back at Watson's side, Krystal said, "I don't like Wakefield's confidence. Could he really have enough pull to get out of this?" She couldn't get Wakefield's boast about controlling members of Congress out of her mind.

"Not if Enoch Whitehall has anything to do about it," replied Strachey. "But he sent the HRT here on his own authority. I'm worried about how the bureaucracy will react."

"Shit." The vision of a villain like Wakefield walking away from his crimes was unbearable. The man was breathtakingly malignant as though with his every exhalation he spread a terrible infection.

"Still," continued Strachey, "there's no denying the crimes he's commited. There are too many witnesses and too many corpses. It would take something extraordinary for him to escape the consequences."

Watson heard them and piped up. "I swear if I still had my gun I'd shoot him on the spot, just on general principles."

"I'm with you there, buddy," said Strachey

The medic approached and addressed Watson. "Do you think you can walk outside? We have vehicles to take us to the copter. I can arrange a stretcher if you prefer."

"I'll walk out of here on my own two feet," said Watson. Just don't let me get too close to Wakefield."

"No problem there, sir." He turned to Strachey and Krystal. "You might as well come along with us so you can stay with your friend."

"What about my car," asked Krystal. "It's parked back on the main road about a mile from here."

Hearing her question, the AIC said, I'll have someone drive it back. May I have your keys, please?"

The way he said it left no doubt that she would have a helicopter ride that night, and she wanted to stay with Frank anyway.

The medic helped Watson to his feet and Krystal and Strachey followed them outside where two black

SUV's were parked. The outdoor floodlights had been turned on, and the front of the house was bathed in light surrounded by the dark woods.

The team leader stood by one of the SUV's speaking into a microphone. He turned toward them and said, "We have two choppers waiting in the field over there," he jerked his head to the north. "We'll be leaving in a few minutes."

"Please make sure Wakefield isn't on our helicopter," said Strachey. "We might be tempted to toss him into the bay."

The team leader cracked a thin smile. "Don't worry. Good guys on one chopper, bad guys on the other under guard."

The front door opened, and they all turned to watch Wakefield, hands cuffed behind his back and flanked by two guards, each holding him by an arm, step out. They were leading him down the steps when Wakefield's head jerked back and he sagged in the guards' grasp. The guards let go of him and brought up their weapons. Wakefield dropped to the steps and lay there without moving.

One of the guards shouted, "Shooter," and everybody took cover.

There had been no sound, and Krystal had a hard time processing what was happening. Hunkered down behind the SUV with the others, she asked, "What the hell is happening? Are there more of Wakefield's men out here somewhere?"

"Impossible," gritted the team leader as he scanned the dark tree line. "We got them all."

They waited there, covered by the bulk of the SUV for what seemed like a long time, but nothing happened. The AIC gave an order, and the HRT moved in a line toward the woods, weapons at the ready.

A tall man wearing black combat fatigues and carrying a rifle fitted with a telescopic sight and a silencer emerged from the other side of the woods. He moved fast and quietly, though he limped due to an old war wound received in Afghanistan.

The team found nothing in the woods but reported hearing a car driving away at high speed.

Everybody congregated around the inert figure of George Wakefield sprawled face down on the steps. Closer now, they could see that the back of his head had been blown away where the bullet exited. The team leader cursed under his breath.

"So much for delusions of grandeur," said Strachey.

Watson caught up with them. He took a look at Wakefield's destroyed head and said, "'The body of a dead enemy always smells sweet.'"

Everyone stared at him.

"Titus Flavius Vespasian," said Watson. "Famous saying. I'm beginning to feel a whole lot better."

Accustomed to Watson's seemingly endless supply of homely aphorisms, Krystal was for once speechless.

CHAPTER 32

Two days later they were all assembled around the conference table in Enoch Whitehall's office.

Not much had been said during the flight from St. Michaels to Quantico. Along with some of the HRT, they'd shared the helicopter with Katherine Dillon who sat with a white face all the way with her arms around her children.

Watson was led away to receive medical attention while they were invited to wait in a visitor reception area. Krystal approached Katherine gingerly. There was still much to be learned from her.

She took a seat beside the widow. "Do you feel up to talking right now?"

If the eyes are the window on the soul, Katherine Dillon's soul was distressed. It would take considerable time for her to heal the wounds of the past few months. But that she had a brave spirit was attested by her having made the phone call to Alex Apelbaum that eventually broke the case. There was resilience in those eyes, and some anger, too.

She answered in a weary voice, her eyes not leaving her children. "They don't understand what's happened. It's all been a sort of adventure for them, staying at home and playing games. At least that horrible woman didn't mistreat them."

"Can you tell me what happened that first night when Dugan went out?"

It was painful for her, but Katherine answered. "Dugan received this call. He seemed to recognize the voice, but he didn't say who it was. The conversation was short, only a minute or so, and then he got dressed and rushed out."

"Did you know what was bothering Dugan?"

"He knew Wakefield was working for the Russians. The more he learned about what his father and George Wakefield were up to, the angrier he got. He confronted his father and demanded he drop the Wakefield account, but Paul refused. The money was too good, he said. Dugan thought he had an ally in Wakefield's organization, and I've always believed it was that person who called him out to the meeting. Dugan was careful, so it must have been someone he trusted."

"When did the Russian woman come to your house."

"It was strange. She rang the bell only a few minutes after Dugan left. I thought at first he'd returned and forgotten his key. But that woman barged in, and she was carrying a gun. She's barely let me out of her sight since. She said the children would be harmed if I didn't do as she said."

So Dugan Dillon had been doomed from the moment he took the phone message. His murderer had already set everything in place. "Why did you call Alex Apelbaum? Why him?"

Katherine was puzzled. "Who?"

"Alex Apelbaum, the editor of the All The Truth website."

"Oh. I didn't know his name. Dugan gave me the number even before that terrible night and told me to call if anything happened to him. I think he was planning to give the whole story to All The Truth.

"Why them?"

"Dugan was into sites like that – conspiracy theories, anti-establishment stuff. He'd been active in college, but hid his feelings from his father after he joined the firm. All the news in the press about Russians interfering in our elections really set him off."

"Thanks, Katherine, you're very brave to have made that call. I'll leave you alone now, but we may want a word with you sometime later."

Katherine turned her attention back to the children.

Everybody spent that night at Quantico where they were assigned to some unused student quarters. Next morning they were driven back into Washington directly to 935 Pennsylvania Avenue, better known as the J. Edgar Hoover Building.

The "dragon" ushered the three of them into Whitehall's office where Strachey was surprised to see Harvey Grant waiting for them with the FBI man. He didn't know if this was good or bad.

CHAPTER 33

Harvey Grant returned Strachey's stare with a Sphinxian smile but said not a word as Whitehall invited everyone to take a seat around the conference table. To Krystal's eye nothing had changed in the office since her last visit over a year ago. The nearly anonymous space was still as gray and sterile as its resident.

Grant and Whitehall took seats next to one another, and Whitehall distributed single sheets of paper to the three visitors. Strachey glanced at his and snorted. He'd seen such documents many times in a former life. "Non-disclosure agreements," he said.

"Yes, Mr. Strachey," said Whitehall. "A legal formality, but quite necessary in this instance. The three of you have been involved in a very complicated and highly compartmentalized matter of national security. If you read the document you will see that the penalty for disclosure of what we are about to tell you is quite severe."

In silence they signed and dated the agreements and passed them back to Whitehall who told them Grant had something to tell them.

Grant cleared his throat. "The CIA has been aware of Wakefield's activities for some months now thanks to a new source inside Avraham Golubov's organization in Moscow. However, knowledge has until now been strictly limited to only a few officials and no action has been taken for several reasons. The FBI was, of course, informed at my insistence, though the information was shared only with the Director of

Michael R. Davidson

the FBI and Enoch. A few White House officials also knew."

Strachey interrupted to ask why nothing had been done if they had all the information and had identified the guilty parties.

With a sad shake of his head, Grant sighed as though he thought the reason should be obvious. "Why, Bob, we had to protect our source in Moscow. Also, the very idea that members of the House and Senate could be subverted by the Russians is abhorrent. Should such knowledge become widespread, confidence in the Government would be destroyed. The number of compromised individuals is relatively small, less than a dozen, but they sit on both sides of the aisle, and it takes only a few to pass or reject legislation."

Krystal was puzzled. "But the press has been full of stories about how the Russians are interfering in the election. Everyone already knows about the hacking and publication of information. It doesn't seem like much of a secret."

Grant agreed and reverted to spook-talk. "Yes, that's so, but we think that part of it is only a diversion - what the Russians call *maskiovka*. The subversion of legislators is much more subtle and has permanent consequences beyond a single election. The more spectacular and generally known activities are meant to keep attention away from their true objectives."

Strachey said, "In a town where leaking has become a major pastime, it's amazing nothing has come out."

"Yes, Bob," replied Grant, "That's a masterpiece

of understatement. And that's precisely the reason for such strict compartmentalization and lack of aggressive action. Can you imagine the public reaction if members of Congress were suddenly arrested for espionage? It would reverberate down the years, and the system might never recover. We've debated for months about what could realistically be done."

"And then Dugan Dillon was murdered, and we began an investigation," said Krystal.

Whitehall fixed his gray eyes on her. "We couldn't be certain at first, but we knew the Dillon firm was tight with Wakefield, so we watched as your investigation progressed. But nothing happened until that Internet article appeared. That made us nervous. We didn't know how much Alex Apelbaum knew and feared he might reveal more than just Wakefield's connection with Russia."

"And then he was killed along with his partner," breathed Krystal. An icicle of suspicion pierced her chest as a new thought struck her – *a government-sponsored assassination?*

Whitehall read her thoughts. "Oh, it wasn't us. Despite what Hollywood would have you believe, we don't go around murdering people for political purposes, least of all American citizens."

"And neither do we," added Grant.

"At least not in the U.S.," jabbed Strachey, who knew a thing or two about foreign operations.

Grant gave him a sharp look. "Quite so, Bob, at least not in the U.S."

Whitehall hastened to continue. "Apelbaum and his partner were almost certainly killed on

Wakefield's orders, or perhaps Moscow's. I doubt we'll ever know. But your investigation shifted to Wakefield, which meant you had to be closely monitored. At the same time we thought it would be a good thing if George Wakefield could be brought up on murder charges rather than as a Russian agent of influence. So we watched what was happening. I apologize, Krystal, but we also separately contacted Chief Heck and requested that he support your efforts despite any political pressure that might be brought to bear. He is not aware of the full extent of the matter, but he did as asked like the good soldier he is."

That explained a lot. Heck knew he had backing against all those harassing complaints. Krystal had never suspected. But it annoyed her. "Why didn't you just bring us in, too? It would have made the job a lot easier. Bob was nearly killed."

Whitehall accepted the rebuke. "We considered bringing you in, but in the end we decided it was best to permit your investigation to continue independently."

"If that's so, why did you try to warn me off, Harvey?" asked Strachey.

"Because of who you are, Bob." Grant was somber. "Your training and experience is significantly different, and your instincts could well have led you to the right conclusion. We wanted the police to continue with a straight homicide investigation because it had the potential to remove Wakefield from the field without blowing the extent of Russian penetration."

"He figured it out, all the same," said Krystal, still annoyed. "We were pretty certain we were dealing with espionage. But then you called me to that meeting and confirmed our suspicion when you told me about that Russian lawyer."

Whitehall nodded. "Yes. Harvey and I saw that you were entering very dangerous territory. We did not coordinate our action with any of our principles. FBI and Agency leadership, as well as the White House, were on pins and needles and by then actually hoped to stop you going any further. On the other hand, we two had come to the decision that inaction would no longer serve. It was quite possible that nothing at all would be done, and we needed a catalyst. You provided it."

Krystal's ire was rising. "What it provided was our being captured and set up to be killed." She'd never before expressed anger toward Whitehall, but the FBI man had hidden important facts from her and she and Watson had stepped into a nearly fatal trap.

Strachey laid a restraining hand on her arm. "The confrontation in St. Michaels was because of what happened at Paul Dillon's house. There was no way anyone could have predicted that. What we did then was because we feared what might happen to Katherine and her children. We made that decision, Krystal, not Mr. Whitehall or Harvey."

Strachey was right, but it was still hard to tamp down her anger. "So why are you telling us all this now?"

"Because," said Grant, "we think you deserve to know everything. It's thanks to you that action is finally being taken. And, of course, the non-disclosure agreement."

Whitehall continued, "With Wakefield out of the

way, his organization will be quietly dismantled and the PACs he financed will be closed. Thanks to Harvey's source, we know the identities of the compromised politicians, and they will be discreetly but firmly informed that their elective careers are over. They will be encouraged not to stand for re-election and to find reasons to leave office immediately. In the meantime their every action will be closely scrutinized."

"But none of this will ever become public," said Strachey.

"That is correct, Mr. Strachey," said Whitehall. "Wakefield's demise will be officially reported as an accident. His surviving accomplices will be given swift, quiet trials and sentenced accordingly."

"What's to keep them from talking?" asked Watson.

"They will be sentenced accordingly," Harvey Grant repeated Whitehall's words.

Strachey thought he knew what that meant. "Do you still have some black sites, Harvey?"

There was no reply.

"What about Paul Dillon?" asked Krystal. "He was in on everything Wakefield was doing."

"Paul Dillon should be jailed for his crimes, but it won't happen," said Whitehall. "He, too, will retire never to be heard from again."

"So that's it?" asked Krystal. "We're supposed to pretend nothing happened?"

Whitehall replied, "I'm afraid the Dugan Dillon murder must be placed among the cold case files."

Krystal felt cheated. It had not been too far off base to suspect she and her friends were being used by Whitehall as pawns. They had been pulled inexorably into a vortex of murder and intrigue with no chance whatsoever of a clean resolution. Had their efforts been in vain? No, Wakefield was dead, and Katherine Dillon and her children were safe.

Robert Strachey was worried about something else. "What's to keep the Russians from exploiting the situation. With no more equities at stake, they have a lot of ways to get information to the public. If they do, their objective of destroying faith in the government will be achieved."

"That's another question entirely," said Grant. "There are back channels we can use and threats we can make – stronger and broader sanctions, arming the Ukrainians, among others. Time will tell."

"That's not very reassuring," said Strachey.

"There are no guarantees, Bob, and you should know that," said Grant.

"I'm afraid I know it all too well."

Watson summed it up. "I don't know about y'all," he drawled, "but I feel like I'm caught between a dog and a fire hydrant."

CHAPTER 34

"I think I'm gonna quit."

"Hmmm?" Ray Velazquez rolled lazily onto his side to face her. "Am I that bad in bed?"

She whacked the side of his head. "I'm not going to quit THAT. I mean Arlington."

He propped his head in one hand, definitely listening now. "Really?"

Outside Ray's bedroom window the mid-morning Miami sun was beginning to do battle with the city's air-conditioning units. They'd enjoyed a late night on South Beach, and neither felt guilty for lazing in bed on a Saturday morning. "Really," she repeated. "I've been thinking about it for a long time."

"Do I have anything to do with it?"

"Yeah, but that's not the only reason."

"Care to elaborate?"

"It's just that I'm not happy there anymore. There's a stench around Washington that I can't get out of my nostrils."

"It's really that bad?"

"I can't tell you." But she wished she could.

"OK, let's say you quit. What would you do?"

"I haven't decided."

"You could move down here. I know Dade County would hire you immediately. In fact, I can guarantee it."

"I dunno. Moving from one police department to another doesn't seem so attractive."

She read the disappointment on his face and quickly added, "But I do like Miami."

This cheered him. "So what are you thinking of doing?"

"I've had an interesting job offer."

He raised his eyebrows and waited.

"I could spend more time down here, maybe even move here permanently."

The fact was that Robert Strachey had decided to set up a private security and investigation business, and he wanted her to be part of it at a salary three times what Arlington County paid. It would mean a huge change from the existence she'd known most of her adult life.

She was considering the offer seriously ...

THE END

Michael R. Davidson

ACKNOWLEDGEMENTS

I must thank the remarkable Jacqueline Beard of Wales, UK, for smoothing out the many errors in the earlier manuscript of this book. She is the ultimate proofreader and the final authority not only for me, but for several other writers of whom I am certain you are aware.

The Author

Michael R. Davidson was raised in the Mid-West. Heeding President Kennedy's call for more young Americans to learn Russian he studied the language, and military service took him to the White House where he served as translator for the Moscow-Washington "Hotline." His language abilities attracted the attention of the Central Intelligence Agency, and following his military service Mr. Davidson spent the next 28 years as a Clandestine Services officer. Seventeen of those years were spent abroad in a variety of sensitive posts working against the Soviet Union and the Warsaw Pact. In the private sector he worked as a business owner and security and economic development consultant before devoting full time to his writing.

Michael R. Davidson